Journey

Through

Thorns

By

Donald Morrison

Published by Dark Forest Publishing

ISBN 978-0692549834

Designed by Donald Morrison

The
Author

"Inspiration strikes like lightning. This bolt's for you, Mr. Kendrick Shen."

- Donald Morrison-

For the last two years Andrew Miller prided himself on being that father that would be sitting at the kitchen table cleaning his shotgun when his fourteen year old daughter; Claire, brought her little boy friends over to visit. He relished the thought that the high school she went to teemed with hormonally charged, pubescent boys that were too afraid of Claire Miller's dad to try and get in her pants. He loved it. But now she was a junior, and after lengthy conversations with his wife, Sharon, and countless nights lying awake with the thought of some skeevy teenage punk sweating on top of his little angel, he could no longer fight the inevitable. His daughter was dating, and there was nothing he could do to stop it. But that didn't mean he couldn't control it.

Andrew woke up to the sounds of his wife and daughter giggling from the kitchen. He couldn't make out what they were saying, but he wasn't born yesterday; Claire's junior prom was weeks away. They were talking about boys.

He pulled himself out of bed, his feet coming to rest on his padded slippers, the ones he took off habitually, in the same spot every night. He slid his feet

1

into the warm embrace and stood up, making his way to the bathroom for a quick shower, and an even quicker shave. After he was done he got dressed and made his way down to the kitchen.

As he entered the room the laughing stopped.

"Morning hon," his wife said.

"Morning Dad," Claire followed up.

"No need to stop on my account," he said with a smile, moving forward to kiss his wife. "I used to be a teenager once too remember."

"Yeah," Claire responded. "But that's when there were still dinosaurs."

"Hey now!" he said, shooting a smile to his wife. "Remember, your mothers just as old as I am..."

"Andrew Miller!" she responded with a snap.

He slapped her lightly on the butt while moving past towards the coffee pot that was still in the process of filling. He grabbed his cup, filled it and then took a seat at the table while his wife finished preparing the sandwiches he would take with him to work.

"K," Claire said, stepping over to bend down and kiss him on the cheek, "gotta go." She grabbed her bag from the chair next to his and said, "Don't wanna be

2

late for class," and then turned to run out the door.

He yelled, "What about your lunch?" but she was already gone.

"She hasn't taken a lunch to school for almost a year now Andrew," Sharon said, placing his wrapped sammies in the tupperware container he used to transport them.

"I know," Andrew said, "but can't a father pretend his daughter's still his little girl?"

Sharon walked over and leaned down, kissed him and smiled. "She's growing up sweetie. Pretty soon she won't be our little girl anymore; she'll be a full blown woman."

"Ech," he responded, flashing a mock look of disgust, "Don't remind me." He paused, taking a sip of coffee. "I miss the days when her biggest fascination was frogs, and watching the horses in Griffith. Now it's all, boys and twitterbook and... ech."

Sharon smiled really big. "It's Facebook honey."

"Eh, whatever," he responded, "you know what I mean."

She walked over and stood behind her husband, putting her arms around his neck. "We knew this was

3

going to happen eventually Andrew."

"I know babe," he said with a heavy sigh, "I just didn't think it would be so quick."

Sharon gave him a squeeze. "She's very lucky to have a father like you sweetheart." She let go and made her way back to the counter, downing the last of her warm coffee. "Look honey, I gotta get out of here, early meeting, but you have a good day ok, and try not to sit here all morning killing yourself over this yeah."

"Yeah," he responded, taking another sip of his own.

"See you later hon," she said, kissing him on the cheek and making her way out the door.

He sat at the table finishing his coffee, and when his cup was done, got up and made his way to Clayton Security Enterprises; the nine to five he had spent the last twenty years supporting his family with.

"Let me ask you a question Jim," he said to the overweight guard sitting next to him at the desk. "If Janeane was starting to date, how would you deal with it? I mean, how do you come to terms with knowing some little shithead's gonna try and take your little girl's innocence?"

"That's easy," Jim said, pulling his pistol out of his holster and cocking it, sliding a shell into the chamber with a solid clack.

"Tch, I wish," Andrew said with a smile.

"Look man," Jim said, unloading the chamber of his pistol and holstering it, "there's nothing you can do about it, but that doesn't mean you can't keep an eye out on her."

"You mean like, follow her..?" Andrew asked, the idea beginning to grow in his mind as he said it.

"We do get paid to do that for a living," Jim said. "Just tail her on her first couple dates, make sure the guy's not a creep."

Andrew nodded.

"You know she's not gonna stay a virgin forever right," Jim said, flipping the monitors to a different view.

"Yeah, but I was at least hoping she'd hold off till she was like, I don't know, forty..."

Jim laughed. "I feel the same way with Janeane man, don't worry."

"Yeah," Andrew said, "just makes me nervous."

* * *

Andrew was laying in bed that night; Sharon's head on his chest, when she looked up at him and said, "I have something to tell you, and you have to promise not to get upset."

He leaned his head back and looked at her. "Should I be scared?" he asked, squinting his eyes.

"I already gave my permission, please don't be angry, but Claire's little boy friend Max asked her out on a date Friday night, and I told her it was OK, but she has to be home by nine."

"What..?" he said, scooting up on the bed into the sitting position. "Why didn't you ask me?"

"Cause I already knew what you'd say. You'd say the same thing you would say for the next ten years if you could." She did her impersonation of his stern voice, "I don't think you're ready for dating yet, I think you should give it a few years, and, boys are evil, disgusting little creatures that only want to sleep with you, and then break your heart."

He sighed. She was right.

"I just worry about her," he said, putting his hand on top of her head; running his fingers through her hair, "I don't wanna see her get hurt."

6

"I know babe," she responded, her eyes closing from the strokes of pleasure. "We've all been hurt at one point, but it's those experiences that make us stronger, and smarter."

He sighed again, sliding back down and pulling her head back onto his chest. "I love you angel," he whispered, leaning over to kiss her forehead before letting his head rest back onto his pillow and drifting off to the quiet embrace of slumber.

The next two days went by, and Andrew tried to pretend like it wasn't bothering him that his daughter was going out on her first official date. When Friday morning bared its teeth at him from behind the screaming alarm clock on the bedside table, he steadied himself for morning conversation he was about to have, and went over his evening plan again and again, replaying the endless scenarios in his head.

"Morning sweetheart," he said as he stepped into the kitchen, after his momentary pause behind the hallway entrance.

"Morning daddy," Claire responded, pausing as she grabbed a banana from the counter. "Look," she began, as if she had been reading his thoughts, "I know you're uncomfortable about tonight, but Max is a sweet boy. He's not going to try anything funny, trust me, his dad's a sheriff, and he'd kill him if he found out he did anything."

Andrew took a deep breath. "I'm just concerned for your safety sweetie, it's a really... messed up world out there."

Claire smiled. "You can say fucked up dad, I'm sixteen."

He smiled. "Don't let your mother hear you say that, she'd kill me."

"I'll be fine," she said, emphasizing the point that she could still smell the worry coming off him in vapors.

"I know, I just have to be a dad sometimes, and that means worrying about his little girl."

She gave him a big hug and said, "I love you too dad," and then turned around to grab her bag and run out the door, yelling bye as she did.

The door closed, and Andrew stood there for a moment before saying, "Bye sweetie," and then yelling up to Sharon, "All right hon; off to work."

He grabbed his security jacket and made his

way to Clayton where he sat and observed others' lives through a series of monitors for eight hours, tracing the movements of the unknown people that made their way past his twelve, ten by ten fields of vision.

The day seemed to drag on and on, and by the time his shift was over he was already packed up and ready to go. He had brought his small binoculars, a small, handheld long distance monitoring device, and an outfit he had purchased the day prior on his way home so that his daughter wouldn't recognize him. He had even gone as far as to buy a Clippers hat, he knew that would seal the disguise, he hated the Clippers, so there was no way she would associate him with that hat.

As he made his way to his car he called his wife and told her he was going out with Jim for a couple beers after work. He knew she didn't believe him; that it was too coincidental that the first time he was going out in months just happened to be the night of his daughter's first date. "You guys have fun tonight," she said, "don't drink too much, and be safe OK."

"Always," he said, opening the trunk to his car and placing his 9 millimeter inside its locking case.

"And honey," she added before ending the call,

"try not to let her see you yeah, she actually thinks you're trusting her."

"I have no idea what you're talking about," he said, a small grin splaying across his face as the love he felt for Sharon flared.

"Uh-huh..." she replied. "You think I don't know you by now."

"Bye sweetheart," he said, hanging up the phone and slipping it into his pocket as he made his way to the front seat. He had about an hour before Claire would be meeting up with Max.

Max. What a stupid name, he thought to himself as he started his car. He chuckled to himself as the image of a boy dressed in brown pajamas with a long bushy tail and a crown danced in his head. *Owooooo!*

He pulled out of the parking lot and drove a few blocks from the Americana; the outdoor mall they were going to be meeting at.

Then he parked his car and changed; made his way to the mall, and found a nice spot on the fourth floor of the elevator structure overlooking the large courtyard shopping area. He waited, and less than thirty minutes later he saw Claire, his angel, his innocent sweetheart, walk into view and make her way to the large fountain in the middle and pull her phone out. Five minutes later a young boy with comb over hair and super skinny pants walked up.

He watched as they hugged, taking note of how long they embraced, which was approvingly quick.

They chatted for a moment and then made their way to one of the outdoor restaurants in the courtyard. That's when he took his cue and made his way down to ground level.

He walked into the Apple store and pretended to browse, keeping his eyes on the pair as he picked up different laptops and put them back down.

After about twenty minutes he decided it was time to change posts; maneuvering his way to a little coffee stand, putting their table just in reach of his audio monitoring device.

He sat there listening to them talk about school, and how much so and so sucked, and how much Mrs. Whatsherface was a total bitch. He had listened in for about fifteen minutes, sipping away on his coffee and taking in the overactive voices through his hidden ear

11

bud, when he noticed the older man sitting across the patio. He was wearing a classic, *Van Helsing* style hat, with a light, weather worn, brown dinner jacket, and was watching Claire and Max intently.

Andrew noticed that he was writing in a rather large notebook; an unusually large notebook, more of a book than anything else. He shifted his focus to the man that was writing; a heavy, uneasy feeling settling deeply into his chest. The man seemed to only take his eyes off of the pair long enough to shoot a glance towards the coffee stand that Andrew was sitting in front of.

He sat there, watching the strange man stare at his daughter, anger beginning to build in him, and just as he was about to get up and say something, his wife's words flashed through his head. If he made himself known, it would be a very long time before he would be able to regain the trust it would destroy with Claire.

He took a deep breath and resolved himself to simply watching, reminding himself that he would be there when they left, and that he would die before anything happened to his daughter. He would keep her safe at any cost.

After a while they finished their meals and

12

made their way towards the mall. It was only seven, so they still had about another hour. Andrew watched as they got up and left, making note that the man stayed there long enough to shoot another glance in his direction, and then made his way towards the other side of the courtyard.

He followed Claire through the mall, watching as they made their way in and out of shop after shop, laughing and chatting the whole time. It was about another half hour before they made their way back to the street, to the waiting cab. As he watched the cab pull away he took his phone out and called his wife.

"Hey babe," he said, watching the yellow caprice turn around a corner. "If Claire isn't at the house in a half hour, I want you to call me OK."

"OK hon. Everything all right?" she asked, beginning to sound concerned.

"Yeah babe, just being dad."

He made his way home and tried to put the strange man out of his thoughts.

Over the next few days he thought about it occasionally, but after a week or so he had all but forgotten; then came the second date.

13

Claire was going to see a Saturday matinee with Max again, whom Andrew had awkwardly met two days prior, when he had picked Claire up from school so that she could pick up her prom dress from the store downtown.

He offered to drop them off at the theater, and then made his way to a parking lot a few blocks away and purchased a ticket to the film on his phone, making sure to get a seat near the back corner. He waited until about twenty minutes after the movie had started, giving time for the previews to run, and the focus to be on the screen, not the new arrival walking in late.

He made his way inside, bought two hot dogs and found his seat. He silenced his phone, and then settled in to watch a two-hour teen film about a vampire love story.

He was scanning the audience for Claire's telltale red hair when he noticed the wide brimmed, Aussie style hat he immediately recognized as the hat that the man who had been watching the pair on their first date had worn.

He traced the angle of the man's brim, and followed it to directly where Claire and Max were

14

seated. He felt his pulse begin to increase, and his hands balled into steel fists.

You have got to be fuckin' kidding me... he thought silently to himself. *No way...*

He sat through the movie and watched as Claire and Max made their way to the lobby amidst the stream of patrons. He sat and waited until the man folded his book and made his way out of the entrance near the screen. He gave a count to ten and then decided it was time to have a chat with him, and made his way to the front, and out the door the man in the hat had exited.

He stepped out into the empty alley, his eyes moving from right to left. The man was nowhere to be seen.

"Where the hell did you go?" he asked himself quietly in the darkness, the orange dirt encrusted bulb washing the cement corridor with its iridescent glow.

He made his way down the alley to the street and looked both ways. There was no sign of the man. He turned, and half sprinted back to his car; jumped inside and peeled out, pulling out of the parking lot and making his way to the front of the theater, where he saw Claire and Max waiting with their sodas in hand, laughing about something or another.

They got into the car, and continued to talk about the movie, and how awesome the effects were, and the impossibilities of a human having a relationship with a vampire or werewolf.

He dropped Max off, said his goodnights, and then started his way home.

"Have you noticed anyone strange following you?" he asked after five awkwardly silent minutes. "Like an older guy with a hat?"

"No..," she replied. "Why?"

"It's nothing," he said, politely lying, in order to avoid scaring her, and not to look like he was being paranoid. "I just saw some weird guy watching you when you came out of the theater."

"Probably just some creep," she responded, slightly calming his nerves with her casual reply.

That night he told Sharon about the guy, and how he had seen him twice now, and how he was watching Claire, and writing in some strange book.

"I don't know babe, I'm getting a really bad feeling about it," he said as he was getting ready for bed. "I mean, this is the second time I've seen this guy watching Claire, and writing in that damn book."

"You're probably just being paranoid honey," she responded, taking her glasses off and setting them on the nightstand. "You know L.A.'s a small city. How often do we run into people we know?"

"Yeah," he responded, crawling into bed, "but this is different. That guys up to something, I can feel it."

"Well," she asked, rolling towards him, "what do you suggest we do?"

"I don't know." He paused, taking a deep breath. "I'll talk to Jim about it tomorrow, see what he suggests. Part of me just wants to run up and grab the guy and be like, why the fuck you following my daughter, but the other part says, what if I'm just trippin?"

"Well," Sharon replied, sleepiness starting to bleed through. "Do that then."

He lay awake for the next half an hour thinking about the man, and scaring himself with thoughts of Claire not coming home one day, or ending up dead on the side of some road, or naked in the woods somewhere, bound and gagged. He beat himself up for not catching the guy, for not being able to say anything, but he also realized Sharon might be right. What if it was just coincidence? What if she just reminded the man of someone he knew; a granddaughter or something? But why was he in a teen movie? It made no sense...

When he awoke the next morning he got ready, ate a quick breakfast, and then made his way to Clayton. It was his day off, but he needed to talk to Jim; he had been driving himself crazy all morning.

He walked into the building and headed straight to the monitoring station they worked. Jim turned around as he entered, and with a surprised look on his face said, "Get your days mixed up man? You know you're not in till tomorrow right?"

"Yeah," he replied, "I have something I need to get your advice on."

"Well," Jim responded, taking the ear bud out of his ear, and turning his chair around, "if it's important enough for you to come down here on your day off, I'll do the best I can."

Andrew grabbed a chair and sat down. "Look man," he started. "So you know I've been following

Claire on her last couple dates right?"

"Yeah." Jim replied.

"Well the last two times I've followed her, I've noticed this old guy. He's been at the last two places she went out to, and he just sits there and stares at her while writing in some big ass book." He paused, taking a deep breath. "I'm starting to get a little freaked out."

"Have you approached him?" Jim asked, now concerned.

"I tried." Andrew responded, his eyes glancing to the monitors out of habit. "Last time I saw him was at the movie theater. I waited for him to leave, but when I followed him into the alley he was gone, like he fuckin' vanished into thin air."

"Have you thought about calling the cops?" Jim asked, shrugging slightly as he did.

"What would I say?" Andrew responded quickly. "There's been some old guy writing in a book and staring at my daughter the last two times I've followed her on one of her dates. They'd tell me to contact them when I had something real to report."

"Well," Jim began, "you could try following him. Don't let him out of your sight, and confront him when he gets to where ever he's going."

"Yeah, but what the hell am I supposed to say; I think you're following my daughter, keep your creepy old ass away? I'd come off like a nut job."

"Better than doing nothing," Jim responded.

Andrew took a deep breath. "I guess you're right," he said, standing up to leave. "Thanks man."

"No problem Andrew," Jim said, turning his head back to the monitors. "It's probably nothing."

"I hope so," Andrew said, turning to leave.

The next day Andrew called in sick to work. He had four days a year that he was entitled to call in the day of work, and be excused from duty; he took this one.

He played off his usual morning routine, and asked Claire what she was planning to do for the day. She told him that she had to spend the morning studying, but at two o'clock, she was going to meet her friends to go pick out their shoes for prom. He smiled and said, "OK," and then made his way out the door.

He went to the local hardware store and purchased a new pair of black gloves, the kind with the latex finger grips which allowed for extra grip in moisture, and coincidentally, the lack of fingerprints. He didn't plan on violence, but when it came to child predators, you could never be too sure.

He called up Jim and told him that he was going to need to borrow his car for the day, that his was gonna be in the shop, and then drove over to his house, parked a couple blocks away and walked the rest of the way. He drove Jim to work, and then shot to the local café, where he hung out at for the better part of his morning, reading the news on his tablet, and working his way through a Stephen King novel he had purchased on Amazon Prime.

When two-thirty rolled around he turned off the tablet, got up, made his way to Jim's car, drove back to his house and parked a couple blocks away.

It was another twenty minutes till Claire's friends arrived.

He sat in the car with the windows down and waited for Claire to run out and jump in the car, and then slouched down as they drove past, kicking the engine on and flipping the car around to follow loosely behind.

They drove to Glendale and parked in the mall

21

structure. He parked a few spots away and waited until they got out of the car and were headed inside to get out and follow. It was not long until he saw the stranger.

The man was sitting in the food court, watching the group as they ate their pizza slices and laughed amongst each other. He was sitting a ways away, staring at Claire, and writing in the book.

Andrew watched from the balcony, hatred building up inside of him as the man eyed his daughter with a predatory gaze.

I will fucking kill you if you try and harm my daughter, I swear to God. Jim's thoughts were a violent squall of aggression and angst. He had to force himself not to jump the balcony and start beating the man into a gelatinous pulp.

The girls hung out for a while, and then made their way into different shops, Andrew watching the entire time from the safety of the upper floor, the old man moving every so often to stay within eye's sight of the group; ceaselessly writing in his tome.

When they had finished up, they made their way back to the garage, got into their car and left.

Andrew noticed that the man did not follow; instead, he made his way to an extremely old Volvo, got inside, and then started downwards, to the ground floor.

Andrew sprinted as fast as he could to the next floor down, and his friend's light blue Prius. He got in and started the engine, nearly squealing the tires as he made his quick exit to catch up with the man he was now convinced was a pedophile.

The man made his way to a house in the hills above Pasadena, in a small community below Eaton Canyon. Andrew followed him the entire way, and then drove past as the man entered a driveway, and parked two blocks up.

He sat in the car for the next three hours, watching the house, and waiting for it to get dark; he didn't want the neighbors to be able to get a good look at him if things went south.

When it was eight o'clock on the dot, and the quiet veil of night had blanketed the sky, he got out of the car, made his way to the trunk and opened the locked case, pulling his 9 millimeter Glock out and inserting the clip into the handle; loading one in the chamber and sticking it into his belt and pulling his shirt

23

over it.

As he approached the house he thought about the consequences of knocking on the door, or ringing the bell. There was no way he would be able to confront the man on his porch without the entire neighborhood getting involved, and that would most assuredly lead to the police showing up, especially in the community he was in. No, he would have to confront the man inside his house, which meant not announcing himself. He needed to break in, and being as though the only light that was on, was coming from the upstairs room, he imagined he would be able to at least get inside without being noticed.

The street was quiet as he walked up the driveway and approached the door. He slowly grabbed the knob and turned; it opened.

He made his way inside, and closed the door quietly behind him, pulling the gun from behind his back and turning to inspect the surroundings.

From floor to wall there were bookshelves. The entire living room was one giant library, book after book, endless volumes that all looked like the book the man carried with him. He walked over and read the

24

writing along the spines; all simply people's names written in gold script.

What the? Andrew thought, as he looked over volume after volume, more than he could count. *What is this?*

After a moment he pulled his gaze from the bookshelves and slowly started towards the stairs that led upwards.

He made it to the top of the stairs, and turned the hallway when a shape emerged from out of nowhere.

Andrew jumped, leveling the gun and pulling the trigger at the same time. There was a flash of light and a loud crack as the gun ignited the air in front of him just long enough to see the frightened face of the man, and red mist as it erupted in front of him.

"Fuck! Fuck!" he shouted, immediately quieting himself and pausing to listen for noise coming from outside; the shouts of people that had heard the shot.

There was nothing; it was silent, save for the labored breathing and pounding of his heart.

He approached the man and leaned down. He had shot him directly in the forehead. He was well beyond death, which had been granted to him instantly.

The smell of gunpowder and burnt flesh wafted up to his nose, and he stood up quickly, turning his head to avoid retching in the hall.

What have I done? he thought. *Oh my God... I'm going to fucking prison.*

He realized quickly that he needed to find evidence that the guy was a pedophile, so at least he had reason for being inside his house. He could make up the story that the man had invited him over, and then attacked him afterwards; nobody cared about predators.

He walked down the hallway towards the only room with light coming from it, and when the glow washed around him, stepped inside.

In front of him was a room just like the first he had entered. It was lined from floor to ceiling with books, thousands of them. His eyes scanned the rows, and then he realized that every one of them had a different name on it, and that they were in alphabetical order.

He quickly followed the rows to the letter M, and then traced down to C.

"Claire," he whispered, stepping forward to pull the book from the shelf. He opened the cover and his heart began to beat even faster, his mouth drying immediately, and his hands beginning to quiver under the weight of the book.

Inside was Claire's entire life story. It started at her birth, and followed her through every major event she had ever had; her first steps, her decision to eat the plastic grapes that had sent her to the emergency room when she was three, her first period, the decision to start dating Max, everything.

Andrew stood there, flipping through page after page of his daughter's life, and then took a deep breath, closing the book, and opening it up a few pages from where the writing ended.

If she decides to go with the blue-strapped Steve Madden's, they match the bracelet she will be wearing, she will save some of the money she has to spend, and when she leaves, she will stop at the gelato bar for ice cream. She will run into the other young boy she has an interest in, Kyle. She will have to make the decision between Max, and Kyle. If she chooses Max, she will travel the world, experience different cultures and

27

become a strong, independent woman. If she chooses Kyle, she will go to college, graduate, settle into a relationship and have three children, becoming a loving housewife, where she will live out her days taking care of her family. If she decides on the purple Aldo shoes, they go a little better with her dress, she will head straight home, and will end up spending her life with Max.

Andrew stared at the words, his head swimming with waves of vertigo. "Oh my God," he said, dropping the book to his feet and turning to run when a folded slip of paper fluttered out from the ruffling pages. He saw his name written in the script that filled the book with Claire's story and froze. Slowly he bent to pick up the piece of parchment, holding it for a moment, staring at the fresh ink before slowly opening it and reading the letter written inside.

Mr. Miller: You were never supposed to see me. Your observant and protective nature allowed for you to glimpse that which should not be. I am one of many referred to as The Authors. As long as man has been, we have watched, each assigned to hundreds, to write your life's stories. Now that I am dead, I can no longer continue those I have been assigned, your daughter Claire's included. Her story, along with hundreds of others now ceases to continue. This was never supposed to happen. I am truly sorry.

He stared at the scribbled note; fear welling up inside him, and then turned and darted down the stairs.

He ran to Jim's car and made his way as fast as he could without getting pulled over to his house. As he turned the corner to his street, a nervousness he had never felt welled up inside him and his jaw fell open, sweat immediately breaking out across his forehead.

The street was lit up with flashing red and white lights; ambulance lights.

He skidded to a stop and jumped out of the still running car, dashing headlong towards the house. As he made it ten feet away from the front door he saw the stretcher.

"What happened!?!" he yelled as the paramedics started making their way down the stairs.

Then he saw his daughter.

Claire was on the stretcher, her arms at her side, IV's already taped in place at her wrists, a clear liquid filled bag attached, and being carried by one of the paramedics.

"Sharon!" he yelled.

"Oh my God!" he heard, as Sharon made her way out of the door behind the medics. "Where the *hell* have you been?"

"What happened?" Andrew asked, watching his daughter being carried towards the waiting ambulance.

"We were in the kitchen, and all of the sudden she just dropped to the floor. It was like, somebody flipped a switch, and she just, turned off." She wrapped her arms in front of her as sobs began to warp her words. "I tried to wake her up but she wouldn't respond. I couldn't reach you, so I called 911. I am so scared Andrew."

Andrew turned to look at the ambulance, a realization sinking into him as he did. "Sharon?" he asked, turning her to face him. "How long ago did this happen?"

"Eight fifteen," she said. "My reading timer had just gone off."

Andrew felt the world fading away, and his legs turning to soft rubber beneath him. He allowed gravity to gain the victory and let his knees give way to the pull, falling into a loose sitting position as they did.

"Andrew!" he heard Sharon yell from a distance. "Andrew! Somebody help!"

The world faded to a static white, and when he opened his eyes, he was staring at the corrugated ceiling of a hospital room, and Sharon was sitting next to the bed he was lying in.

"Wha… What happened?" he asked through dry lips.

His wife stood up and walked slowly to his side. "You fainted sweetheart," she said, grasping his hand softly.

"Claire?" he whispered, trying hard to swallow the dry mucus that had caked the back of his mouth.

A tear worked its way down Sharon's cheek. "She's in a coma."

"What..?" Andrew asked, tears welling up in his eyes.

"They've run every test they can," she said, her other hand covering their grasp. "There's nothing wrong with her, she just won't wake up."

The pail behind his eyes tipped, and he began sobbing heavily. "I did this!" he cried. "I did this. Oh

God..."

"No sweetheart," Sharon said, trying desperately to comfort her distraught husband. "You didn't do this. You couldn't have."

His sobs became quiet, turning into shaking, and an endless flow of tears. He had done it. He was the one responsible. He had killed the man that had been writing her life's story, her Author. It was because of him that the old man couldn't continue her story. It was because of him that she was now doomed to inanimate rest, unable to wake from the eternal slumber now caused by the discontinued narrative. He lay in bed, comfort coming from the woman that would hate him if he ever told her the truth, knowing that there was no way of ever telling her what had happened, and knowing that she would never believe him if he did. He lay there, the sterile hospital room surrounding him, knowing that his desire to protect his daughter, was the thing that destroyed her. She was gone, and for the rest of his life, he would be the only one to know why. Outside, from a window across the street, an older man watched, only pulling his gaze away long enough to scribble something down in the book sitting in front of him.

"If you prick us do we not bleed? If you tickle us do we not laugh? If you poison us do we not die? And if you wrong us shall we not revenge?"

-William Shakespeare-

"911, what is your emergency?"

"911, what is your emergency?"

"911, hello?"

"They're dead..."

"Look, I'm gonna get help on the way, could you tell me who is dead?"

"It's my family. They're all dead."

* * *

When the police showed up at the Ryan residence, fifteen-year old Toby was sitting on the front porch, his head hung down, gaze locked to the ground between his feet. Not once did he look up, even when the police were helping him carefully into the back seat of the cruiser.

* * *

"NO!" Kelly yelled. "It's mine!"

Kelly was Toby's older brother. He was three years older than him; manipulative and spiteful, even for his age.

"Please," Toby asked, his voice timid and small, a whisper beneath his brother's rage.

"Give it, back!" Kelly yelled, yanking the small racecar out of his hands, and dropping it in the process.

The plastic car had been a present for his brother's sixth birthday. It wasn't extravagant; the kind that would wind up when pulled back, and whiz off for ten feet before needing its repeated tug of acceleration.

It hit the floor and cracked. So did Kelly. He looked at his younger brother with vengeance and fury burning behind his hate-filled eyes and brought his leg up, kicking his little brother hard in the chest, sending him tumbling down the last four stairs to the dining room entrance. As Toby collided with the hardwood below, his arm flung out and connected hard against the end table that held the lamp his grandmother had left his mother when she passed away. It wobbled precariously for a moment, and then lost its delicate fight with gravity, crashing to the floor below and shattering into a thousand pieces.

Toby lay on the floor, tears welling up in his eyes, a stifled cry beginning to work its way to the surface of his lips when his mother called out from the kitchen, "What the hell is going on in there?"

Then the tears began.

"What the fuck did you do to my lamp!?" his mother yelled, walking across the floor in his direction.

"Do you have any idea what that thing meant to me you little shit!"

Toby sat there crying in a heap. His arm hurt badly from the fall, and his chest hurt from where his brother had firmly planted the ball of his foot.

His mother reached down and grabbed him by his arm, the one that was throbbing, and yanked him up.

He screamed.

She drug him down the hall to the bathroom and flung him inside. As he crashed to the floor his head hit the base of the toilet with a crack. His vision blurred, and his head began to swim.

"You're gonna stay your little ass in here and think about what you've done, and I swear to god, if you make one sound..."

Toby was already starting to fade from consciousness as his mother slammed the door and stomped down the hall.

When he woke up, his head was pounding, and there was a small trickle of drying blood that had worked its way down his forehead just above his brow line. For the next two hours he sat in the darkness of the bathroom sobbing quietly, his little head resting on the soft sleeves of his pajamas.

* * *

The police had cordoned off the house, and there was a thin strip of yellow plastic running the perimeter of his front yard. Toby's head was leaned back against the hard plastic of the cruiser bench, and his gaze had fallen out the window to the house.

It was dark, and the flashing lights ignited the front of the white two-story house in a dazzling display of reds and blues. The surrounding neighbors had all made their way out of their houses, and were beginning to crowd on the outskirts of the tape, all quietly chatting amongst themselves.

He stared blankly, watching as policemen chatted in front, and two men dressed in white coveralls made their way into his house. His mind was a silent scape, and the sounds of the world around him blended into a faint buzz inside his ears.

* * *

"Ugh, ungh!"

Toby heard the sounds coming from the hallway. He recognized his mother's voice, but could not recall hearing her make those sounds before. He knew his brother and sister had gone camping with their uncle for the weekend; he was still too young to go, so he had stayed home with his mom and the man who had started living there early that year, his new daddy as his mother had told him.

"Oh god, Oh fuck!"

He made his way into the hallway and slowly started down the hall. He didn't know what he was supposed to do if she was being hurt, he was little, and still afraid of the dark, so if someone was hurting her, he didn't know what he could do to help, but he had to try.

He crept down the hall slowly, approaching the door to his mommy's bedroom and reached up for the knob.

"Oh Jesus!"

He slowly turned the knob and pushed the door open. When it was about half way, he saw his mommy sitting on top of his new daddy. She was naked and moving back and forth, riding him like he'd seen the other kids ride the horses in Griffith Park. "Mommy?" he said, checking to see if everything was ok.

"Jesus Christ!" she yelled, grabbing the sheets from around her and covering herself up.

The man pushed her aside, and she tumbled to the floor. He got up, naked and walked quickly to the door, saying loudly, "Jesus Marie, lock the fuckin' door would you!"

The man used his foot to push Toby hard into the hallway and slammed the door.

As the door slammed shut, Toby's head impacted the wall behind him and stars burst into his vision, accompanied by a high-pitched ringing sound in his ears.

His little body slumped sideways to the carpeted floor, and his vision faded to a starry black.

When he woke up the house was quiet again, and he crawled back to his bedroom, pulling himself up onto his bed, and softly tugging his GI Joe sheets up to his chin.

His head was throbbing, and the ringing in his ears had yet to stop. If anything it had gotten louder, more persistent. He felt nauseous, and lay there most of the night, staring at the ceiling, and the bluish white lights that flittered in front of his eyes, dancing across

41

the air.

* * *

"Hey Jim, Coroner's here."

The officer standing in front of the car nodded, and then approached the man that was walking up from the van that had just parked in the street.

"Hey Bill," the police officer said, sticking his hand out to shake that of the arriving man's.

"How many we got Jim?" the coroner asked, his gaze falling to the house.

"Four," the officer replied. "One in the kitchen, one in the downstairs bathroom, one in an upstairs bedroom, and the other in the shed out back."

"What are we looking at here?" the coroner asked, referring to the cause of death.

"Um…" the officer started. "I think you better have a look for yourself."

"That bad huh?" the coroner said, turning to make his way to the house with a stretcher; a large black bag laying across the length of it.

* * *

"Oh my god Jenny, he is like, way too young."

Toby

Toby's sister had convinced their mother to let her have a sleepover. She had invited three of her good friends from school, and they had decided to have some amusement at her little brother's expense. He was ten years old now, and his sister had noticed him looking at her friend Amanda. This had given her a good idea, so now Toby was sitting in the room with them, while his sister convinced her friend to take her clothes off to make her little brother blush and see how long it told for him to run from the room.

"Oh come on," his sister said. "He's never seen a pair of boobs before. Why don't you show him what girls are all about?"

"I don't know Jenny," her friend replied nervously. "It just feels, weird."

Toby sat there on the edge of the bed, wondering what they were talking about, smiling happily about being able to hang out with his sister and her friends.

"He's gonna see em someday anyways," his sister said with a smile. "Might as well be from the girl likes. Ain't that right Toby?" she said, turning to him as she did.

"Um…" he responded shyly, not knowing how to answer.

"You're fucked up, you know that right?" her friend said, standing up from the chair across the room, and slowly walking towards Toby as she did.

"You know," she said, stepping towards him and unbuttoning her blouse as she did. "You're kinda cute."

"Oh my god!" her friend snickered from the other side of the bed.

The girl bit her lip and slowed her pace until she was standing just in front of him. She swayed her hips back and forth, and let her blouse slip delicately to the floor at her feet, and then reached behind her back and unsnapped her bra.

"Is this what you want to see?" she asked, letting her bra slip down just a bit.

Toby sat there nervous, a feeling coming over him that he couldn't explain. It felt like his head had gotten light, and there was a nervous anticipation coursing through him.

The girl bit her lip again and smiled, letting the bra drop to the floor. She slowly caressed the underside of her breasts and moaned. That's when Toby saw what was happening below.

"Oh my God!!" her friend said loudly. "His dick just got hard."

He looked down, and a feeling of shame and embarrassment washed over him. Instantly his face was hot, and he wanted to run from the room.

"Oh, disgusting!" his sister yelled. "You little pervert!"

She reached over to the desk and grabbed the small bucket with melted ice in it that they were keeping their sodas in. "You need a cold shower," she said, dumping the bucket of freezing water over his head, splashing down his back and legs at the same time, drenching the corner of the bed and the floor.

Toby screamed from the blast of cold water that had just been dumped across his bare skin.

"Oh my God!!" her friend yelled.

"What in Christ's name is going on in there?" their mother yelled, stomping down the hallway as she did.

"Oh shit!" his sister said, pushing Toby to the floor and dropping the bucket as she did.

Their mom swung the door open, and her eyes

dropped to the floor, and then saw the water splashed everywhere. "What in the hell is this!?" she snapped.

"It was Toby," his sister said. "He came running in here and tried to throw a bucket of cold water on us."

Her fiery gaze locked onto him as he sat shivering on the floor, still stunned from the blast, and the embarrassment of what had happened with his special parts. She stepped forward and grabbed him by the arm, lifting him to his feet, and walking towards the hallway, pausing to tell his sister, "Get that god damn mess cleaned up, I don't want mold growing under the carpet," and then shut the door behind her and switched her grip to his hair.

She pulled him down the hallway by his scalp, his feet trying to keep up with her pace as she did, and then she swung the bathroom door open, and flung him inside, his body crashing hard to the linoleum, the door slamming heavy behind him as the darkness surrounded him.

* * *

Toby stared at the front door as the coroner made his way slowly out, a body now filling the black bag that had gone in empty.

"Jesus Jim," he said as he approached the car. "You weren't kidding... I have never seen anything like that before, and I've been doing this job for almost forty years now." He paused, glancing at Toby as he did, lowering his voice. "What the hell happened in there Jim?"

"I don't know Bill, I don't know..."

* * *

Three months after the incident with the water, Toby's brother turned thirteen. For his birthday their stepfather had allowed him to get a pellet gun. He had been told to be careful, and that if he hurt himself, or anyone else with it, it would be taken away, and given to Goodwill. "It's for cans and squirrels," their stepfather had said.

A few days later Toby and his brother were in the back yard. His brother had set up a couple of tin cans, and some action figures on the fence at the edge of the yard. There was some scrap metal piled up against it, and some loose wood below. They had been pretending that they were invading an enemy fort, and that they were elite snipers with a special unit.

Toby had asked if he could shoot, but his

47

brother had snapped quickly, "NO! It's mine, and you're too young anyways."

He had contented himself to watch, and had even agreed to play spotter, telling his brother to shoot a little to the right or the left, depending on where the pellet hit.

They had been out there for about twenty minutes when his brother aimed at a small army figure on top of a metal post. He aimed carefully and fired. There was a ping sound, and all of the sudden the gun dropped from his hands, and he froze, a small trickle of blood starting to fall from his forehead.

The pellet had ricocheted off of the post, and came back at him. His brother stood there shocked, and then realized that his stepfather would take his new gun away if he knew what happened. He glanced at Toby and said, "If you tell on me, I'll cut your eyes out with my knife, you hear me," and then began pretending to cry loudly.

Moments later their stepfather came walking out the back door and yelled, "What the hell's going on out here?" He walked up and saw the blood coming from Kelly's forehead and asked, "What in the hell happened to your face?"

Without hesitation he turned and pointed at Toby. "Toby asked if he could shoot my gun, and then he pointed it at me and pulled the trigger." He lost himself in a series of theatrical sobs as their stepfather looked at him, his features tightening. Then he locked his gaze to Toby. "Boy, I'm gonna teach you a lesson you are never going to forget." He grabbed him by the arm and drug him inside, closing the door behind him and pulling his belt off at the same time.

For the next three minutes he laid into Toby's butt and lower back with the one inch thick piece of leather. The more he screamed, the more his stepfather hit him.

Eventually he stopped when he saw blood, and then picked him up under his arm and carried him upstairs to his room where he dropped him on the floor just inside and turned around, slamming the door shut and locking it from the outside as he did, cursing as he made his way back down the hall.

* * *

Toby's gaze moved to the upstairs window, and the room that used to be his brother's. His jaw clenched

49

tightly, and his eyes quivered for a second before his features relaxed again, and he let his gaze soften.

The coroner made his way back up the walkway to the front door, his stretcher once again empty, save for another large black bag.

* * *

Six months had gone by, and his brother had one of his friends over. He was supposed to be babysitting while their parents went out for dinner that night. He had told Toby to come hang out with him and his friends in his room, that they had brownies, and that they were pretty good. He said they were going to play video games and hang out, and that he'd get to stay up late. Toby was ecstatic. He rarely got to stay up after his bedtime, and especially not hanging out with his brother.

He was sitting on the floor of his brother's room, his two friends were sitting on the bed, and his brother was pulling a small bag from inside his closet.

"Look man," his brother's friends said, "I'm not so sure this is a good idea. The dude said these were pretty strong."

"I know," his brother replied, stepping back

from the closet with a grin, "that's what's gonna make this even better."

He pulled a brownie out of the paper bag and handed it to Toby with a smile. "Here you go little bro. You're gonna love this."

Toby smiled and took the brownie. "Thanks Kell," he said, biting into the semi-sweet chocolate.

"Awww," his brother's friend said, "Kell."

"Hey, fuck you," his brother said.

"This tastes kinda funny," Toby said, looking at the brownie as he did.

"It's just a different kind of chocolate," his brother replied. "These ones are special."

For the next half hour they all hung out, playing video games, Toby sitting on the floor listening to his brother and his friends laugh and talk. All of the sudden he began to feel really funny. His head got really heavy, and his jaw began to quiver. It felt like his skin was crawling and he began to get really scared. "Kell," he said, fear in his voice. "I don't feel so good."

His brother smiled at his friends and stood up. "Don't worry Toby, I've got something perfect for you.

He walked behind his bed and grabbed a large

plastic garbage can and walked up behind him, dropping it over Toby, and then telling his friends to grab the weights from the floor, and piled them on top of the can.

Toby screamed as everything went dark, and pushed as hard as he could against the plastic. No matter how hard he pushed it wouldn't move. He screamed and cried, pleading for them to let him out, but there was no reply. He heard laughing, and the sound of his brother's door closing. Then he was left alone to the sound of his breathing, and the dull hum of the video game system running in the background.

Three hours went by before he heard his brother's door open and the voices of him and his friends. He heard him walk up, and shuffling coming from the top of the can. His body hurt badly from being cramped in the position it was in, and not being able to move, and his breaths were coming short and shallow. It had gotten hard to breath, and the air was quickly running out. He had gone past the point of being scared, and had wet himself.

When his brother pulled the garbage can from off of him he asked, "so what did you think of the brownie?" This was followed up with a loud laugh.

"Oh Jesus Kelly," his friend said, noticing the wetness on the front of Toby's pants. "I think he pissed himself."

"Aw, nasty," his brother said. "Get the hell out of here. God. Now my room smells like piss."

He pushed Toby who was still feeling sharp pins sticking throughout his legs, and was dizzy from the rush of air.

Toby hit the floor, and then with an extra boost from his brother's foot against his backside, made his way into the hallway where he crawled into his bedroom and fell asleep on the floor, his pants still warm with urine and sweat.

* * *

"Look at you, you fuckin piss pants pussy."

Toby's stepfather stood over him glowering down.

He had a nightmare, and for the first time since he was a little boy had wet the bed. He had been on his way to the bathroom to clean up when his stepfather had walked out into the hallway and caught him with the front of his pajamas saturated.

"Twelve years old and you're still pissing the fucking bed." He paused, shaking his head in disbelief. "Man, your father must have been a fucking retard. I heard you're the reason he's dead."

Toby felt like he had just been kicked in the stomach. He felt sick, and beyond the point of tears.

"If it wasn't for you, your daddy wouldn't have gone out for cough medicine that night, and wouldn't have crashed his car." He paused, nodding his head. "So how's it feel to know that you're the reason your dad's dead huh?" He scoffed. "Shit, if I'd a been him, I'd have rolled over and shot your ass at the wall in the first place, specially if I'd a known you'd a been such a god damn pussy."

* * *

The coroner walked out with another body on the stretcher, pausing as he approached the officer guarding the cruiser. "You know, I think I might just have to retire after this one."

"Tell me about it," the cop said. "Looks like the whole damn family went and fell off the deep end."

"Yeah," the coroner replied. "But I ain't ever seen anything like this... This is more than just suicide.

These people must have decided to go out in the most painful way possible, cause that.., that's a whole nother level…"

* * *

The summer air was warm, and there was a cool breeze blowing past. Toby was sitting on the front porch of his house listening to his parents argue inside.

As he was watching the street in front of him, movement caught his eye. Just up the block, walking slowly down the sidewalk was a stray tabby cat. He looked at it, and watched as it got closer.

He heard the rumble of an engine and turned his head in the other direction. Halfway up the block was a large white moving van. It was heading fast down the street.

Toby's gaze fell back to the cat, and his eyes narrowed.

The cat paused, its head turning in the direction of the porch.

The cat stared at him for a moment, and then Toby broke its gaze, looking to the moving van and then back to the cat. His pupils began to dilate and the cat stopped in its tracks. It held his gaze for a moment, and then just as the van was about to roar past, stepped out into the street, and into the path of van's tires.

There was a crunching sound as the wet splatter of remains were flung from the back of the van and came to rest a few feet away.

Toby sat on the porch staring at the mangled remains of what only moments ago had been the passing cat, watching the blood slowly pool itself outwards.

* * *

The coroner made his way out of the house and down the walkway. This time there was no exchange between him and the officer. He seemed dazed, and his eyes were locked to the ground in front of the stretcher as he slowly moved past towards the van.

* * *

Two years had gone by. Toby was now fourteen. He was sitting alone in his room staring out the window at the tree growing in their front yard. His expression was blank, and he felt nothing but hatred coursing through him. Every fiber of his being was filled with an unbridled rage that was beyond verbal description.

He could hear his sister talking from the other room about some guy she was seeing, and how he was in college, and how huge his cock was, but to him it was just a screeching blare, sharpened fingernails grating down his spine.

The urge to spit came over him, and he clenched his fists till his knuckles hurt.

He could hear rock music coming from his brother's room, and the smell of pot coming through the vents into his.

His mother was in the kitchen starting dinner, and he could sense that his stepfather was in the toolshed behind the house.

The black void of hatred had swallowed him, enveloping him in a suffocating shroud, and everything had faded away lest the pounding of his heartbeat in his ears.

* * *

The coroner entered the house again, and as Toby's gaze fell back to the front door that now stood open, another officer walked up. "Detective Daniels."

"Captain," the detective replied.

"So what do we got here?" the captain asked.

The detective took a deep breath. "Suicide. Four victims, a mother, father and two kids. We have one survivor, the youngest, a boy; fifteen. Apparently the older brother used a buck knife to scramble his brains through his right eye socket, the daughter emptied the racks in the oven, and crawled inside, closing the door behind her after setting it to broil. The father was found in the toolshed out back. He stuck a five-inch drill bit up his nose, and then held the trigger down and shoved. And get this... The mother apparently went into the bathroom, and drowned herself in a toilet full of her own feces and urine."

"Jesus," the detective responded.

"Yeah..." the officer replied.

The detective pulled out a cigarette and lit it up. "And you're sure that this is a suicide detective?"

"The only prints on the knife are the kids', the girl could have pushed the oven door open, there was no forced entry into the shed, and the bathroom door was locked from the inside." The detective paused. "Yeah, as crazy as it sounds, they did this to themselves."

"What about the youngest one?" the captain

asked.

The detective took a pull from his cigarette, lighting his face up for a second. "He's the one that called 911. The officers that arrived on the scene said he was sitting on the porch when they got there."

"No history?" the captain asked.

"He's clean." The detective replied, dropping the cigarette and putting it out with his foot.

* * *

The lab was bright and sterile. It was fourth period, and Toby was sitting through his organic biology class. On the desk in front of him was a frog in a box. Each of the students had one, and they were going over the preparations for dissection the next day.

Toby was staring at the desk that the teacher was standing behind. The frog had jumped out and was edging its way towards the tub of sulfuric acid that was being used to dissolve the flesh of another frog, so that the skeletal structure could be cross referenced in the next day's lab.

Toby had locked his gaze to the frog, and as it was about to jump from the desk, it turned and locked its eyes to his.

Toby felt a tingle of energy surge behind his eyes, and his pupils dilated. The frog slowly pulled its gaze away and walked towards the metal tub, paused, and then jumped into the basin full of acid.

The teacher continued his lecture, his back turned, and the rest of the class was writing notes. No one noticed the frog jumping to its slow, burning, chemical death, or the small grin that escaped Toby's lips.

* * *

The coroner made his way out of the house with the last body. He approached the car and stopped.

"So what's gonna happen to the kid?" he asked the detective.

"Well, we gotta take him to the psych ward. They'll run some tests on him, make sure nothing's wrong, and then if no one comes to claim him, he'll be remanded into state custody, and sent to a boys home or foster care till he's eighteen."

The coroner nodded, saying, "Well, it's all you guys in there. I think I'm gonna need a few drinks after this one."

They said their exits and the coroner made his

way to the van to load the last body.

The detective called two nearby officers over. "All right. Let's get this kid over to Huntington. Shrink'll be there in the morning."

"You got it," one of the officers replied, tapping the other on the shoulder. "Come on."

The police officers got in the car and started the engine.

As they pulled away Toby's gaze was still locked to the house. When they turned the corner his eyes moved to the back of the seat in front of him.

"So what's his story?" the cop in the passenger seat asked.

"Family killed themselves," the other replied.

"What the fuck is wrong with people now days?"

"You tell me and we'll both know," the officer driving said; rolling his window down a crack.

"What about him?" the one in shotgun asked nodding to Toby in the back.

"We're gonna drop him of at the psych ward, and then who knows; probably a juvenile center or something."

Toby's gaze slowly drug itself from the seat back to the men in front, and he felt the familiar tremor of energy behind his eyes.

"Sucks to be..."

Toby's pupils dilated and the officer's words cut off mid-sentence. A quiet calm came over the police cruiser, and then the officer in the passenger seat reached down and unsnapped his pistol, slowly pulling it from the holster and bringing it up to the side of his head. The other unfastened his seatbelt, and then closed his eyes pushing down on the gas pedal as he did.

Toby reached across his shoulder and brought his seatbelt across, clicking it securely into place. There was a small grin splayed across his lips as the front seat erupted in a flash of light, and the shoulder of the road began to creep closer.

THE

BOND

"Grief knits two hearts in closer bonds than happiness ever can; and common sufferings are far stronger links than common joys."

-Alphonse de Lamartine-

Chapter 1

The air was cool in its embrace, inviting yet softly unsettling. The thin carpet of mist swirled around Jerry's feet as he cautiously made his way out of the tree line and into the backyard of the house he instantly recognized as the dilapidated building his grandmother had once inhabited; the one that was still owned by the family, but mainly used as a two-story storage shed in the off highway, tiny town of Alton, Utah.

He edged his way past the frail, picket fence that was making a feeble attempt at cordoning the yard off from the encroaching woods. He looked down and realized that he had an old, rusted shovel in his hand, and that his steps seemed to be moving him forward, a motion that more automatic than conscientious.

He made it into the backyard and stopped. He felt a presence; one of familiarity, one of comfort. He turned his head and saw his sister standing there. She looked cold and afraid. Her arms were wrapped around herself and she was staring at the ground just beyond the back stairs. He had no idea how he knew, but there was something down there; something old, something malevolent and trapped.

The pair made their way slowly forward to the spot that permeated hatred and captivity, and came to rest in place. They exchanged a quick glance, and then Jerry stepped forward and brought the edge of the corroded metal down, swift, and hard against the forgiving earth. As he did, the downward momentum stopped three inches into the soil, and there was a solid *thunk* that seemed to reverberate with a contained echo. He shot a glance back to his sister, and then started scooping the dirt away.

The next twenty minutes crept by with an arduous silence enveloping them, and when they finished they stared down into the container beneath their feet, and gazed upon a sight chilled them past the flesh and veins, straight to the marrow in their bones.

Below them, was a large steel container with a glass top that must have been nearly four inches thick; its walls and floor made of ancient steel that was awash in the colors of oxidation and rust. There was a single space on the cover, roughly two feet by two feet, with a ladder leading downwards, and an old, sturdy key lock held the latch in place. It wasn't however, the container that held their attention in jagged claws, it was what was on the floor that ran their breath short, and caused Beth to move next to her brother, seeking the comfort of his arms around her.

"My god Jerry," she whispered. "What is it?"

"I don't know," he responded slowly. "But whatever it is, it's in pain; agony. I can feel it."

He wasn't an empathetic man; quite often actually, he'd get scolded by his girlfriend for not being able to sense her emotions, but here, in the shambles of his grandmother's backyard, he could feel everything. He could feel the torment and suffering that the creature below had endured, the endless torture of being held below the earth, void of sunlight and living, damned to wander back and forth in its corroded tomb. He looked down at the rotting husk of what had once been a human; a woman from what he could tell, and felt pity stab through him. The sight of the flesh, and the rotted cloth covered skeleton slowly pacing its way back and forth brought tears of unknown sorrow to his eyes. A deep sob threatened to pull from his chest. "We have to do something," he said. "We can't leave it here like this."

Beth's silence signaled her agreement, and he pulled his arm from around her and stepped over to where the dirt encrusted brass lock sat, the small metal warden holding its captive securely below.

He glanced at his sister one more time and then turned, raising the shovel high above his head, and then bringing it down onto the lock.

CLANK!

Again he did it, repeating the process until the metal finally released its grasp and fell free.

Beth stepped next to him, and he took a deep breath, sliding the latch to the side, and flipping the steel lid open with a painful creak.

He made his way down to the rotting corpse, and looked into the black recesses that stared back at him, endless portals to an all-consuming void. As he stepped forward he realized that he didn't feel even the slightest inclination of terror, that even with his fascination of zombie fiction and culture, that here he stood, feet away from the horror he had grown to fantasize about, and he didn't even feel the slightest ping of enmity.

He stepped forward and whispered, "You're

68

free," and then brought the shovel hard against the side of its head, striking it with all his force.

The creature fell hard against the wall it was next to, and then collapsed in a heap to the floor, like a marionette with its strings sliced cleanly through.

He brought the shovel up, and slammed it down, hard into its neck, sending its head rolling to the side, the smallest puddle of blood slowly seeping outwards.

As he did, he heard laughing echoing in the background, slowly getting louder as he spun around, shooting a frightened look up to his sister who stood at the edge, peering down at him through the thick glass, petrified in fear.

It got louder and louder, until it felt like the pressure of the cackles was going to make his eardrums give way with a deafening pop, and when the pressure built to just below that threshold, Jerry Aguilar shot up in bed, his hands shaking; sheets covered in a darkened pool of sweat.

Chapter 2

Jerry lay there stunned, surrounded by darkness; the sound of the freeway drifting in through the window of his Hollywood apartment. His hands were shaking and he felt heat permeating from his body. After a moment he realized he was still breathing like he had just finished a four-block sprint, and he flipped the covers down and brought his sweat-drenched legs to the edge of his bed.

He sat there for a moment, his head resting in his palms with his fingers tucked through his short bed-riddled hair. When he caught his breath he reached out to call his sister; then as if on cue, a ringing began from his bedside table.

With a start he reached out and grabbed his phone, squinting as the lighted screen invaded the small space his darkness-adjusted pupils had allowed. It was Beth, and it was almost three o'clock in the morning.

"Beth?" he said, standing up to make his way to the kitchen for a glass of water.

"Jerry," she replied through the phone. "I just had the worst dream."

70

Jerry stopped in his tracks, the thought of water, and urge to pee fading away instantly with her words.

"Jerry? Are you there?" she asked, not hearing a response. "Jerry?"

"Yeah," he responded after a moment. "I'm here."

"Um, I'm sorry I woke you, I was just frightened. I'll give you a call in the morning OK?"

"It was grandma's house," he said after a moment. "Wasn't it?"

There was silence.

"Oh my God," she responded, barely passing a whisper.

"Look," he continued. "I'm working in Venice tomorrow, one of the schools out there needs an emergency sub. There's a coffee shop right near the beach; why don't you meet me there at say, four?"

"...Yeah," she responded. "I'll do that; and Jerry?"

"Yeah sis?"

"What if it's real?"

He stayed quiet for a moment, not knowing

71

how to form the words that would follow. "I don't know."

He brought the phone down from his ear and disconnected the call. The air in his apartment had taken on a Los Angeles chill, which meant he needed to close one of the windows. He walked over and closed the one nearest his bed, and then remembered his thirst. He walked back towards the kitchen and grabbed a glass from the cabinet above the sink, and then stepped over to the fridge for his Brita filter. When he opened it up, two blackened holes were staring back at him from behind leathery rotted flesh, and the cackling began.

Chapter 3

When Jerry awoke that morning he called his sister.

"Hey sis," he said when she answered her phone. "Got a minute?"

"Sure," she said. "What's up?"

"Look. I had a really crazy dream last night, and I was wondering if we could meet up. I need to talk about it with somebody, and since you were in it, I figured it'd be best if it was you."

"Um, ok? Sure. When and where?" she asked.

"Well I'm subbing at a middle school in Venice today, so how about you meet me at Menotti's off of Windward, say four o'clock?"

"Ok, I know the spot," she said. "Everything all right?"

"I don't know Beth. I hope so."

He hung up the phone and finished getting ready for work. He was a substitute teacher, so preparing for his day consisted of business casual, and a folder full of notes on the subjects the teacher may or may not have been going over; and a small flask of bourbon for if it was one of the classes he had now gotten used to; which was full of students that had a seemingly endless hatred and disrespect for substitute teachers.

Jerry spent the next ten hours trying desperately to fight back the image of the woman in the clear-topped tomb, and her abyssal eyes that had stared at him from inside his refrigerator. The day went by quickly, class after class, one uninterested student after another, until the three o'clock bell rang, and the last of his temporary students made their way hurriedly out of the classroom. He put his things back into his brown leather side bag; *man purse* as his girlfriend called it, and then made his way out to his car.

He kicked the quiet engine of his early model Volvo wagon over, and made his way to the beach to meet Beth.

By the time he had found a parking spot he was already starting to regret calling her. He was going to sound crazy, and the way she'd been acting lately, he felt like he might be making a mistake.

He pulled into a space two blocks from the

shop, and let his hands drop into his lap. He leaned his head back and took a deep breath, exhaling slowly and pausing for a moment before reaching out to grab the broken plastic handle and swinging his heavy door outwards. He shut it with the usual slam it took to get the latch to engage, and then made his way to the shop, the sunken features of the woman's face swimming behind the saddened, pain filled sockets for the three-minute walk in the heat.

When he stepped onto Windward the cool springtime breeze drifted past. He made his way to the cafe and walked inside. He ordered a coffee and grabbed a seat near one of the wall-sized windows, letting his gaze fall to the bustling street in front.

Twenty minutes later Beth arrived.

He stood up and hugged his little sis. She was only two years younger than him, but he still called her his little sister. He ordered an almond milk latte for her, and then returned to the table next to the window, yelling hi to Nicely; the manager, as he took his seat.

"Thanks for coming," he began. "I know I usually call in advance to meet up, but this dream I need to talk to you about has got me on edge." He paused, taking a sip of his coffee and glancing out the window. "I think it might have something to do with grandma."

He now had Beth's full attention. She had always loved her grandmother more than anyone else; their connection unmatched by any other member of their family. She may have been closer to her than even their mother.

"Jerry?" she asked, not having to spell out what she meant by her two-syllable question.

He took a deep breath and began. He told her about the dream, about the zombie woman, the container, how it was in their grandmother's backyard, the phone call, the severed head in the fridge, everything. For the next ten minutes he sat across from her at the table and spewed words that could be coming from a mental patient, or the next Guillermo Del Toro story.

When he was finished they sat in silence for a moment before she spoke up.

"Look, Jer. You know me; I don't think anything happens without a reason. If you're having dreams like this, then they mean something. It may not be grandma, but it's definitely your subconscious trying to tell you something." She paused. "Maybe we should go check on her, I mean, it has been almost a year since the two of us showed up together; it'd probably do her some good."

Jerry nodded. "I just don't wanna freak her out, or get her thinking about death. That's the last thing she needs."

"Jerry," Beth said raising her eyebrows. "She's ninety-seven years old, I'm pretty sure she's already come to terms with the fact that her time is coming to an end. I doubt a few dreams are going to get her going."

"Ok," Jerry said with another small nod. "You wanna go Saturday?"

"I think I can do that," Beth responded with a smile.

"So how you been doing lately?" Jerry asked, taking another quick sip of his warm coffee. "It's been hit or miss with getting you on the phone these past couple weeks. You and Jim doing alright?"

She brought her hand up and ran her fingers through her hair, her gaze falling to the postcard stand in front for a moment, then back across the table at him.

"Jerry." She paused. "I have something I need to tell you, and I need you to promise me that you won't freak out and lose it like you normally do."

Jerry looked at her puzzled. "What's up sis?"

She took another deep breath. "Jerry, I have cancer."

His jaw dropped, and he almost lost the cup of coffee that he was setting down.

"What!" he said, constraining his voice below a shout, disbelief and shock sparking outwards through his words. He didn't know what to say. The air left his lungs and a hollow emptiness laved with pain flooded in.

"It's stage two," she said, still looking at the metal stand. "My lungs."

He felt the heat growing behind his eyes as tears fought to make their way out. "...When?" he asked quietly.

She let her eyes settle into a soft embrace with his. "I found out two weeks ago."

"Oh Jesus," he said.

"They caught it relatively early," she added

quickly. "Or at least that's what my oncologist says. He's got me on minor radiation pills, and in another two weeks, I'll begin chemo treatments."

"Oh please no," he said, shudders running through his chest. "I can't lose you sis," he said, a tear working its way from the corner of his eye. "Not yet, not like this."

She smiled. "I'm not dead Jer. Don't start rolling my casket out just yet. I still have time to fight it, and I'm looking into alternative treatments as well, ones that don't pump you full of radiation and poisons; like this one in San Diego called the Gerson clinic. Apparently they've been curing cancers much worse than mine for years, far more advanced cases through nutrition, so there's still hope."

He felt nauseous, like the world around him was spinning.

"Besides," she said with a smile. "You're the older one, you gotta go first; there's an order to these kinds of things." She reached across the table and clasped her soft hands around his. "I'll be fine Jerry, trust me.

He pulled his hands away and wiped the tears

that had made their way down to his collar away, then reached out and took her hands in his and squeezed. "I love you Beth."

She smiled even bigger. "I love you too Jer Bear."

"Oh fuck..," he said, his gaze falling out the window. He took a deep, heavy breath and exhaled slowly, releasing the sob from the well it was lying in. "How's Jim taking it?" he asked, his eyes slowly moving back to hers.

She nodded slowly. "He's hopeful." She paused. "Look Jer, I'm so sorry to have dropped this on you like this... but I didn't know how to tell you. I'm sorry."

Jerry nodded.

"Look, I gotta go. Jim's at the house with Amanda, and he's supposed to be going to one of his stupid Dodger games, so I told him I'd stay home with her this afternoon. I told him to go out. I don't want him moping around the house. I really need to be around smiles and laughing. If I stop being positive it's over for me, and I need the same from you Jer. You have to help me on this, I need my big brother, and I can't have you looking like a sad puppy every time I see you, you hear me."

Again he softly nodded.

She stood up. "Now promise me you're not going to spend the next twenty-four hours wallowing around that tiny apartment of yours worrying about me."

He took a deep breath and exhaled while nodding, feeling the onset of what was going to become a headache. "I won't."

"K," she said.

"Tell Jim I said hi," he said blankly. "And that I'll try and make it out to one of the games with him sometime this season."

"Ok," she said, turning to make her way out, stopping four steps away and turning back to him. "Hey Jer."

"Yeah," he said, looking up quickly.

"Smile," she said, flashing one at him.

He scoffed lightly, and let a small grin escape. It wasn't one of joy; it was the thought that even when faced with something like this, his little sister could still manage to stay happy.

She turned, leaving him to sit alone at the large

community table awash in fear and now sadness. He finished his coffee and then made his way back to his apartment. When he got there he made a bee-line straight to the cabinet above the fridge that held his bourbon collection, and pulled a bottle of Elmer Lee down and filled an old fashioned glass three quarters of the way, a breath later, it was empty. He corked the bottle and made his way to the couch where he flipped on the television and grabbed his X-Box controller. He wanted to turn everything off for a while, and when it was time to do that, he wrapped himself in the warmth that was his comforting security blanket; video games. He hit play game, and the Capcom logo washed across the screen. Resident Evil. 'How fitting,' he thought to himself as the whiskey warmth began to fill him, and the edge started to soften.

He sat there for the next two hours, killing zombies, and mutated creatures on a derelict cruise ship before falling asleep with the controller in his hand. It was another four before he woke up and turned the TV off, and made his way to bed, groggy from the Elmer Lee that had graciously worked its way into his system.

That night he dreamt of the house again, and

the woman with the empty sockets, filled with a blackness that pulled everything around into them; portals to a world of unending pain and suffering.

Chapter 4

When Jerry awoke the sun was already blasting its way into his room. He got dressed and made his way into the kitchen, for a moment forgetting about the news his sister had told him, and started making himself a breakfast of eggs and this vegetarian chorizo he had come across at the Ralph's up the street from his house.

He had just finished dropping his reddish yellow concoction onto a plate when he heard his phone ringing from the bedroom; it was Beth's ringtone. He set the plate on the counter and nearly sprinted to the bedroom.

"Hello?" he answered quickly.

"Hey Jer," she responded, sounding just as chipper as she always did. "So as it turns out, the meeting I had this morning was canceled. I could be at your place in an hour, wanna head to grandma's then?"

"Um, yeah," he responded. "Let me throw this food down my throat and grab a quick shower, I should be ready by the time you get here. I'll leave the door unlocked."

"Perfect," she said.

He could tell she was smiling; there was a tone that she used that accompanied it, and it made the worry that was setting in seem to dissipate a little more.

"See you in a bit," he said, hanging up the phone to make his way back to his plate of food that looked like it had been pre-chewed for him.

He finished eating and jumped in the shower. He was finishing up when he heard Beth call out from his living room. "Jerry, I'm here."

"Out in a sec," he yelled, grabbing a towel and drying off.

He made his way to the bedroom and started getting dressed when she walked in.

"Hey," she began, as he stood naked in front of his closet, grabbing his clothes. "Sorry I dropped that on you like that yesterday. I guess I should have written a letter or something, but I knew if I didn't tell you then, who knows when I could have. I really didn't have the guts to say it, so when it just came out..."

"It's fine Beth," he said, pulling his jeans on. "I was going to find out sooner or later, so I guess, it didn't really matter where. Not like the setting would have made it any less difficult to hear."

"Guess so," she said, bobbing her head. "Well, grandma should be up by the time we get there."

He knew she would be. For the last who knows how long of her life, she was up like clockwork every morning when the sun came up. "Not enough hours for living," she'd say all the time, and whatever her routine was, it seemed to work. Their grandmother had never gotten sick a day in her life, not even as much as a cold. When they asked how she did it, she just said, "Eat right, and don't be lazy."

Jerry finished gathering his things and they jumped into Beth's car. She didn't like riding in the tank as she referred to his Volvo, "smells like old people and Nirvana."

They headed for Glendale, and forty minutes later they were pulling into the parking lot of the nursing home.

They stepped out the Jeep Beth had fantasized about for years, before finally convincing Jim that they absolutely had to have it, and made their way to the front doors.

As they approached, one of the orderlies was walking another resident out in a wheelchair.

"Hey you two," the man said. "Been a while since I've seen your faces here. Thought you might have forgotten about your ole' grandma."

"No," Beth said, exchanging a smile with the man. "We've had kind of a busy schedule lately."

"That little girl still got you running around like crazy?" he asked.

"Non-stop," she replied, putting her hand on his shoulder as they passed.

"You two have a good day now, and don't let Rose push you around you hear?" He paused, throwing a smile at Jerry. "Jerry."

"Paul," Jerry said with a smile and a nod.

"You as well," Beth replied, opening the door to the home.

They made their way down the first floor hallway. Their grandmother's room was at the end. It looked out into the courtyard, which she had raised such a fuss about wanting, that after two months, they finally made some moves, and got her the room she wanted.

As they walked in she looked up at them from the bed and smiled. "Beth, Jerry."

"Hi grandma," Jerry said, stepping forward to give her a hug.

Beth smiled and leaned down to kiss her on the forehead.

"What brings you two down here?" she asked. "Not that I mind; it's just that you usually call before you come, and to be honest, I can't remember the last time you both showed up at the same time."

"Well," Beth replied quickly, making up a story better than the one that she knew Jerry would respond with. "We both had the day off today, and figured, we haven't come and seen you in a few weeks because of our schedules, so we thought it would be nice to come together."

"It's very nice," she said. "Please, sit down. Can I get you two anything, a drink or a snack? I can hit the button and they'll bring you something right away."

"No," Beth said, shooting a smile at Jerry. "I think we're fine." She paused. "We just wanted to come check in on you and see how you were doing. Is everything ok with you?"

"Of course it is," she responded, shooting them a suspicious look. "What is it *really* that brings you two here today?"

They shot each other a quick glance, and Jerry started, taking a deep breath before beginning.

"I've been having these really strange dreams the past few days. They're extremely vivid, more than any I've had before." He paused. "In the dreams I'm in the backyard at your old house in Utah, and there's this large container. There's some sort of... zombie, or something inside it, and when I kill it I hear this screaming laughter, and that's when I wake up." He paused. "We got kind of worried about you."

Their grandmother's face had turned the color of cold slate, any remnants of blood beneath the skin disappearing. Her hands began to shake, and her eyes opened wide, causing Jerry to look behind him, half expecting to see the dead woman standing there.

"Gramma?" Beth asked, beginning to feel fear building inside her, from the pale vision of her grandmother. "Gramma, are you ok?"

She didn't respond; she just stared at Jerry through petrified eyes.

"Jerry, call the nurse," Beth said from behind him.

"No!" Rose snapped, her gaze flashing to Beth, then falling back to Jerry. "When did the dreams begin?" she asked, seriousness draped over her words.

"Um... last week."

Jerry stood there with his sister behind him, and stared into his grandmother's face as a tear slowly fell down her cheek.

"Gramma, are you all right?" he asked softly.

She took a deep breath, glancing between Jerry and Beth. "It's time," she whispered, slowly pulling herself into a seated position, with the help of the beds remote. "I need you both to listen to me very carefully," she began; slowly adjusting the covers around her legs. "I'm old, very old," she began. "I'm much older than you, or anyone else thinks I am." She paused, taking a deep breath, and lowering her voice to just above a whisper. "I was born in eighteen eighty-one."

Jerry and Beth shot each other a quick glance.

"I'm going to be a hundred and thirty-five years old this year." She stopped looking at her grandchildren. "I feel it. I feel old, and for the last three years, I've been lying here in this home, waiting to die, knowing that eventually, some day, it might actually happen." She paused, letting a small smile flash across her face. "Sit," she said, patting the bed next to her as her gaze pulled away from the patio.

Jerry and Beth took a seat on the bed. Neither could believe what they were hearing, but their grandmother's words were crisp, lucid. And she had never been the storytelling type, so they listened, and listened intently.

"When I was younger, barely into my twenties, your great grandparents and I lived just outside Boston Massachusetts. We lived in a small town that was a stopping point at that time for the gypsy caravans that traveled around the east coast. Well, one day a caravan stopped in town, and I was at the market, selling vegetables." She paused, taking a small breath and exhaling with a sigh held silent. "He was a Romanian boy, a little older than me at the time. He had the perfect smile, and the most piercing green eyes. His name was Boldo, and I knew instantly that I had fallen in love, but there was no way that my family was going to approve of me marrying a gypsy, and his family would never accept me into their clan, so we were forced to try and live a life of love in the few short

91

weeks that they were camped."

Jerry and Beth stayed quiet; shocked from the words they were hearing.

"Those three weeks we spent every moment we could together. We knew it wouldn't last, but we couldn't bring ourselves to think about that."

The afternoon nurse walked in with a lunch tray in her hand. "And how are you doing today Miss Rose?"

"Afternoon Shelly," Rose responded with a smile. "I'm doing fine, still kicking along."

She set the tray down and smiled at Jerry and Beth. "Well, you all have a nice afternoon, and you call me if you need anything ok?"

"Of course," Rose replied with a smile, grabbing the call button next to her bed to emphasize.

She waited for the nurse to leave and then continued. "It was one of the last days before the caravan was going to leave, and Boldo came to me, and told me to meet him in the woods just outside the town as the sun was setting. He said that he had a way that we could ensure that we could be together again, and that not even sickness or plague could take us." She leaned over and took the small glass of orange juice and took a heavy sip, handing it back to Jerry to put back on the tray next to her bed. "I met Boldo in the small clearing we had made love for the first time. He told me of a gypsy spell that would grant me eternal health, and that with it, sickness or disease would never take me, and that way, there would be no question if I would be alive the next time they passed through, and that then, we could leave together, and live the rest of our lives wrapped in each other's love." She paused, taking a deep breath. "There was a catch however, and as it is in the gypsy world, nothing is gained for nothing. He said that for the spell to work, someone I loved would have to give their life, for me to have my health." Her gaze fell to the window; sorrow flushing her face. She swallowed hard and then continued. "It was my sister..."

Jerry stayed quiet, watching his grandmother's eyes. He had never known she had had a sister.

"We had been arguing," she continued. "She knew about Boldo and I, and she'd been threatening to tell our parents about him. If they had found about our late night trysts, they would have locked me in my room and not let me out for weeks. My father would have gone to the Gypsy encampment, and I would have never seen my love again." She paused, her gaze flitting out of the window as her mind graced the features of her long lost Boldo. "I told her to meet me in the clearing," she said, her eyes returning to the disbelieving gaze of her grandchildren. "When she entered Boldo grabbed her from behind and threw her to the ground." She paused again, another tear forming. "I used the knife he had given me and plunged it into her back." The tear fell silently down her cheek. "He had said that the spell had been contained to the blade, and that once her breath stopped, we would have to bury her, and that the spell wouldn't take effect until the dagger was pulled free. He had dug a large hole at the edge of the clearing that day, and built a crude cage from metal scraps and fencing wire. We drug my sister to the hole and dropped her into the open cage. As we rolled her in, I yanked the knife from her back and dropped the cage roof. We covered it with brush and shoveled earth on top of that, using more brush to ensure she would never be found." Her gaze fell to the bed sheets across her lap. "That was the last night I ever saw him..." Another tear. "For the next thirty years I never got sick, even when a flu wiped out over half of the town, and took my parents with it. They never gave up hope that one day my sister would return, that she had just run off, and that one afternoon their daughter would come strolling back in with some tale of a failed love, or daring escape from capture. For the next thirty years I lived with that guilt, until once again I had to face my sin." She took another sip of her orange juice, clearing her throat to continue. "It was after my parents were buried and I had moved to Alton with your grandfather; Joe, that I came face to face with my sister again. They had been building more and more houses near where she had been buried, and the direction they were developing in was going to lead them right to her, so I had no choice but to move her; to bring her home. I went back to Boston, sold the house, packed everything inside of it up, and filled a moving truck with boxes, and my sister, bound and confined to a wooden crate."

Jerry and Beth stayed quiet, aghast at the tale they were hearing.

"I had sent Joe to stay with his sister in St. George for a few weeks. I told him that it was going to be hard for me to go through the boxes, and that I needed to be alone. During that time I had the steel structure built in the backyard; a tornado shelter I'd told the company I'd hired to build it, and for the last ninety years, my sister has wandered in the confines of that steel cage, rotting alone in the darkness that I left her to be forgotten in." She took three labored breaths and stopped. "Please, Beth, Jerry. She's suffered long enough. Please go there and put an end to all this. End this so that she and I can leave this world; so that we can finally rest. I'm so tired of living. Please."

Beth stood up and said, "I'm sorry Grandma," and turned and walked out.

Jerry looked at her for a moment, wanting desperately not to believe her, but knowing; feeling that she was telling the truth.

"What do we do?" he asked sounding like he had just swallowed a handful of Quaaludes.

"You have to go there," she said, reaching out to take his hand in her warm grip. "You have to go here, and you have to release her from the cage she's been confined in, the one made of flesh, not steel."

"And what then?" he asked, feeling the hesitation of wanting to ask wash over him.

"I don't know Jerry, I don't know. I was never prepared for this."

He nodded and stood, making his way to the doorway, pausing before walking out. His mind was swimming with the words she had just poured into him, and the fact that his dreams were more than just that; they were a message.

When he got home he pulled the bottle of bourbon from the shelf and skipped the formality of the glass, pulling the cork and swilling from it like a sea-parched sailor.

He made his way to the couch and stared at his dull reflection in the TV sitting across the room for him and tried to formulate his plan. When he woke up, the sun was creeping in and the carpet smelled of whiskey where the bottle had rolled of his lap and drained onto the floor in the night.

He slowly brought himself upright, his eyes getting larger as he did. He scrambled into his pocket for his phone and dug it out as quickly as he could, hitting Beth's number as fast as the device would allow.

"Hello?" the soft voice said from the other side.

"Beth," he said quickly. "I have an idea. If

grandma used this spell to get eternal health, then we may be able to do the same for you."

"Wha.. What?" Beth asked, confused by his ramblings. "What in Christ's name are you talking about Jerry?"

"Look, she said that she used this spell to get endless health right? So if that's the case, then all we have to do is have grandma kill that thing that used to be her sister, then end grandma's suffering in the same way, with the same dagger, and it could possibly cure your cancer. You wouldn't have to go through chemo or any of that. You could beat this." There was silence on the line for a moment. "Beth?" he asked. "You still there?"

"Are you hearing yourself Jerry?" she asked. "Don't tell me you actually believed what grandma said. She's old Jer, and when people get old, their brain doesn't exactly work the way it used to, there's terms for that Jerry."

"I know," he said. "But what if she's right? What if you can get rid of the cancer? What if you could still spend the rest of your life with Jim and Amanda? Wouldn't you be willing to do anything for that?"

"Look Jer, I gotta go. I have a nine o'clock meeting with my radiologist and I can't be late. I'm sorry Jer."

She hung up the phone, and Jerry's hand fell into his lap. How could he make this work?

He looked at his watch; it read 6:25.

"Shit!" he said, bolting upright and darting for his bedroom. He had to be at the school at eight, which left him enough time to take a quick birdbath and throw his last clean shirt and tie on before shooting out the door and driving quickly to Venice.

The day went by and as he was on his way home his phone rang. It was Beth.

"Beth, hey," he said, answering the phone and putting it on speaker at the same time. "What's up?"

"If we were to do this, how can you be sure it would work?"

There was sadness in his sister's words; he could hear it dripping from the phones speaker on the dash.

"I can't," he replied after a moment. "But I can tell you that she's not lying. That much I can say."

There was a pause on the line.

"I'm no longer in stage two Jerry. It's spreading." She hesitated. "I'm in stage four."

Jerry struggled to maintain composure. "Look," he said. "I have an idea. Meet me at my place, I'm heading there now."

There was a pause before she half whispered into the phone, "Ok."

Jerry focused on keeping the Volvo between the yellow lines, as his mind raced three times faster than the wagon was moving. By the time he parked in front of his building he had worked out a plan, and by the time his sister arrived, had worked out the finer details; or so he hoped."

Chapter 5

"Hey," Beth said as Jerry pulled the door inwards.

He stepped forward and pulled her into a hug. Finally she broke.

"Look," Jerry said; twenty minutes, an icepack and two glasses of wine later. "Saturday you're going to meet me at the care home. We're going to tell them that we're taking grandma so she can pass in the comfort of her own home, surrounded by family. We're going to immediately get on the freeway, and head to her old house. When we get there, we'll dig up her sister, and grandma can end her suffering, then, like she begged us to do, we can put an end to her suffering as well, and in doing so, possibly heal you at the same time."

Beth stared at him. "Do you know what you're saying? You're suggesting that we kill gramma Rose. Have you lost your mind?"

Jerry rubbed his face with both hands. "Beth, she wants to die, and you know that if she could help you live that she'd gladly use her life to do so. You know that."

"We can't kill our fucking grandmother! This is insane!"

"You are both dying!" he said, raising his voice to match the level of hers. "There is nothing you can do to stop that. The moment we kill her sister, or that zombie, or whatever the hell it is, her time will end. If we don't..." He paused. "Think about Jim and Amanda."

"Don't you dare!" she sneered. "Don't you dare bring them into this."

"Please." Jerry pleaded. "We have a chance. There is no other choice."

She stared at him. "And what if it doesn't work? Or what if we get there, and there's nothing there; no container, no undead sister? What then huh?"

Jerry's gaze fell to his feet, and when he looked back up he spoke with the seriousness of a judge passing sentence. "That's a risk I'm willing to take to save you." He paused, taking a deep breath and exhaling slowly. "You're the only family I have, and I am not going to lose you without a fight. I'd hijack a spaceship and fly to the sun if I had to in order to save you."

This time it was her that took the deep breath. "I'll tell Jim that I have to go away for the weekend, one last trip with my brother to the house we used to stay at as kids for the summer."

"K," Jerry replied.

"If we're wrong…" she said, trailing her words off.

"I know." Jerry said, responding to the fears her unfinished sentence were to contain.

That night he lay in bed awake for most of it; nervousness and fear of being wrong tearing at his laboring mind, the unrelenting battery not allowing sleep to take hold until the morning birds had begun their light welcoming songs. When he woke up he called the care center in Glendale and made the arrangements to pick his grandmother up the following morning, and reserved a rental car. Last thing he wanted was his Volvo throwing a rod in the Nevada desert or the radiator blowing because of the heat.

He went through the day on autopilot, and let his good friend Elmer snuggle him to sleep that night.

Chapter 6

When Jerry awoke he shot Beth a text. He told her that he was going to swing by and pick her up at eight, and that they had to be at the care center at nine. That gave them time to hit a drive-through for a quick breakfast and some coffee, and to make it from La Cañada to Glendale.

They said their goodbyes at the care center and by ten thirty were on the road heading to Utah.

"You're taking me there," their grandma said after a very long, uncomfortable silence, "aren't you?" She paused, her gaze moving to meet his in the rear view mirror. "It's ok," she said, her gaze falling to the passing hills, the uniform headstones of Forest Lawn bringing stillness to her. "It was always destined to end like this. I created it; it's only fair that I should be the one to end it."

Jerry stared ahead, his gaze locked onto the road, and Beth's eyes watched the passing weeds on the shoulder, her mind still locked in struggle with the actions she wasn't sure she could perform.

"You mentioned a dagger," Jerry said, breaking

104

another long bout of silence. "Do you still have it?"

"I do," she replied from the back seat. "You remember that knife you always wanted to play with, the one that hung on the wall in the kitchen?"

"Yeah," Jerry responded.

His grandmother stayed quiet.

"You never told Grandpa Joe any of this?" Beth asked after another spell.

"Oh heavens no," Rose replied quickly. "Joe was a good Christian man. If I'd of told him I had used some kind of Gypsy witchcraft when I was younger…" She scoffed. "Oh lord. That would have been the end of everything we had. No," she said after another pause. "Some things are better left unsaid."

It was another four hours till they reached Las Vegas, and another four after that till they pulled onto the two-lane blacktop that led from the I-89 to the little town eight miles away.

"You know," Rose said as they traveled down the empty two-lane. "When we first moved here, there were only ten or so families that lived here." She paused, a smile growing slowly across her face. "There was the Heaton's and the Roundy's, and a handful of others. Around the time I left to come to where my family was at, there was maybe two hundred folks that lived there."

"You're not worried someone could have stumbled across the container in your backyard?" Jerry asked.

"No," his grandmother replied. "Everyone in that town has the respect not to go snoopin' around other people's properties. They're all good Mormon folks there. May be a bit weird in their own rights, but they respect others property, that's for sure. Honest folk."

A few minutes later they came around a curve and the small town opened up in front of them.

They reached the first intersection and made a left, pulling onto a gravel road that took them the equivalent of about three blocks down to where the old house was.

Jerry pulled the car to the left in front of the overgrown driveway and turned off the engine.

"Still remember how to get to this old place huh?" his grandma asked with a grin.

"You remember how much I looked forward to

106

spending those months here; running around like a maniac, riding horses and shooting grandpa Joe's guns? I could find my way here blindfolded," he said with a smile.

"I always hated the fact that we had to use the outhouse," Beth said. "Always wondered why you guys never invested in getting an indoor toilet."

"Oh, we did eventually," her grandmother said, "but it just felt too strange; using the bathroom in the house. We'd been using the outhouse for so long, the toilet just kind of turned into another storage area for us."

Jerry got out of the car and made his way to the house, reaching under the long dead potted azaleas next to the door and grabbed the key. He slid it into the crusty lock and turned it with a strained click. As he swung the door open light filtered through the dust particles floating through the air, giving the small living room the feeling of long forgotten treasure cave. He walked through the small maze of boxes to the kitchen, reminiscing about the summers when he was twelve years old, wearing his grandfather's old beaded, native American headbands and listening to old rain dance songs on cassette, and learning how to reload shells, and do leather working.

He picked up an old photo that was on the mantle next to the kitchen door and brushed the dust off. He glanced to the entrance as he heard the car door close, and then turned his gaze back to the picture. It was of his grandma, Grandpa Joe, him and Beth, and their parents when they were still alive. He could still remember the smell of the backyard when the picture was taken.

"Is grandma coming?" he asked when he saw Beth walking in alone.

"She wants to stay in the car till we're ready. Says there's memories she doesn't want coming back in here."

"She misses grandpa," Jerry said, setting the picture back on the mantle.

"Yeah," Beth replied. "Did you find it?" she asked after a moment.

Jerry moved into the kitchen. "Right here," he said, moving to the stove and reaching up for the simple brass handled blade.

He turned it over in his hands and felt the

weight of the blade rock back and forth. It felt smooth in his grasp, like a piece of gold, weighted and custom made for his hand.

"I always wanted this knife," he said. "Grandma caught me with it one time and I got a scolding I can still remember. Don't think I ever saw her get that angry." He paused, turning the blade over again. "Guess I know why now."

He turned and handed the blade to Beth, who took it reluctantly.

"You sure you can do this?" he asked as the weight shifted to her hands.

She stayed quiet, taking a deep breath and slipping the knife into her belt behind her back. "Let's just get this over with," she said, turning to make her way outside and to the back.

"We need a shovel," Jerry said as they turned the corner.

"Over there," Beth replied, pointing to the tree line just beyond the gate to the trail that led to the next street over.

Leaned against the encroaching thicket was a small handful of yard tools. There was a shovel, the flat

109

kind used for moving dirt, a hoe, and two rakes, one the stiff iron kind, and the other a flimsy leaf raking kind.

They made their way to the standing pile and grabbed the shovel and leaf rake, then returned to the spot Jerry had been dreaming about and stopped.

He stood there for a moment, breathing slowly, feeling his heart pounding relentlessly in his chest.

He shot one last glance to his sister and then raised the shovel over his head and brought it down hard into the earth.

Thunk!

The shovel sank three inches and then hit a solid surface.

Jerry felt his flesh crystalize.

He immediately shot a glance to his sister who was staring at the spot where the shovel had impacted with wide eyes, her pupils dilated, pushing the color back with ferocity.

He changed his grip and began to shovel the top layer away, exposing the thin surface of weather beaten glass below. His dreams had been right.

For the next twenty minutes they scraped and raked the dirt away until all that remained was the perfectly rectangular smooth surface below. Darkness had crept in while they were arriving in the town, and in the dim, tree covered light they couldn't see below the translucent layer.

"Do you have a flashlight?" Jerry asked.

"Uhhh, Yeah," Beth responded, pulling her phone from her back pocket and flipping on the flashlight. "Here you go."

Jerry reached out and took the flashlight, setting the shovel down behind him. He took a deep breath and then brought the light up to bare.

As his eyes focused on the shape below his veins turned to slush and he felt a ripple of fear trickle down his spine. Below them was the still corpse of their grandmother's sister, standing in the middle of the enclosure, swaying slowly side to side as if in an endless battle with equilibrium.

"Oh my God." Beth whispered.

Jerry stayed quiet; he had experienced this many times already. He stepped over to the archaic lock and looked at Beth. "Get grandma," he said as he turned to bring the shovel over his head.

Clank!

He brought the shovel down three times before the lock gave way, and moments after he had finish blasting the quiet woods with his intrusive pounding Beth and their grandmother walked up.

There was silence as the trio gazed upon the walking corpse below, and moments had gone by before their grandmother broke the silence.

"I'm so sorry Karen," she said, tears running down her cheeks as Jerry looked at her. "I should have released you long ago, but I didn't have the courage to come back."

Beth and Jerry stayed quiet as they realized their grandmother was sharing her last words to her sister, who had stopped in place.

"You did nothing to deserve this," she continued, stepping forward, her gaze locked below.

Jerry saw that as she spoke, her sister seemed to almost recognize her voice, and strained her neck to bring her two blackened abysses upwards.

"For decades I have left you here, to rot in this underground grave." She paused. "I'm here today to release you. You will never forgive me; you cannot, but there's no need for you to suffer anymore." She turned

112

her gaze to Jerry and nodded.

He reached down and grabbed the hatch, pulled it open and set it down with a soft thud.

As he crawled into the space he could feel something ancient underneath with them, something older than the corpse swaying in front of them, something darker.

His grandmother made it down the ladder with their help, and when the three were standing there, Jerry handed her the shovel. She stepped forward and whispered, "I'm so sorry Karen," and then swung with the agility and strength of a woman much younger than her at her sister's head. There was a crack as steel connected with bone, and the side of her sister's head collapsed inwards on itself, and her body collapsed to the floor.

Beth and Jerry watched as their grandmother stood over her sister and brought the shovel down on her neck, severing her head from her shoulders. Then Beth stepped forward with the dagger in her hand.

"I'm sorry grandma," she said, plunging the blade in her grandmother's back just to the right of her spine.

There was a soft sucking sound as the opened flesh formed around the sunken blade, and her grandmother turned to look at Beth.

"What have you done!?" she asked, a tear forming at the bottom of her eyes. "What have you done?"

Beth stepped back as her grandmother stumbled forward.

Jerry began to step forward as their grandmother fell to her knees.

"This is not a gift," she whispered through a small series of coughs. "Not... a gift..."

She collapsed to the floor, and the pair stood there staring at their grandmother's unmoving body for a moment before Beth rushed to Jerry and wrapped her arms around him, spilling her tears down the front of his shirt.

They stood there for a long while before Jerry said, "We should go," and started towards the ladder. "You have to take the knife," he said as his hands grabbed the rusting rungs.

Beth turned and made her way slowly to her grandmother and bent down, grabbing the blade and

114

slowly pulling it out with both hands.

She stayed kneeled there for a moment before rising to her feet and making her way to the ladder, and back up to the yard and her waiting brother that had the flat head shovel in his hand.

She set the knife down and they spent the next half hour silently covering the container with the two corpses inside. They then made their way back into the house and washed the blood from Beth's hands and the dagger, hanging it back above the stove where it belonged.

The drive back to Los Angeles was quiet. For the next eight hours they spoke only long enough to ask if the car needed gas, but other than that, the conversation was unspoken, and unheard. There was little to say; much that happened needed to remain that way.

When they got back home Jerry dropped Beth off at her house and made his way back to his. He walked into his apartment and passed the beckoning bottle of booze; residing to his bed. There was no woman in his dreams that night.

Chapter 7

The next two days went by, and he heard nothing from his sister. He had returned to work, and the forced ignorance of teenage youth, and coffee that carried him through his day. It was at the end of that second day when he received he phone call from Beth. He was sitting on the couch nursing what felt like the onset of a cold with a cup of chamomile tea when his phone rang; it was Beth.

"Hello?" he said, picking up the call.

"Jerry," she began. "It's gone."

There was a pause.

"Uh, what's gone?" he asked, coughing into the napkin he was holding.

"The cancer."

"What? You're serious."

"Yes Jerry. I came from a meeting with my radiologist today. They ran blood tests two days ago, and a CAT scan. It's gone."

"Oh my God," Jerry said. "Oh my God."

"Yeah!" she replied. "It worked Jer, it really worked. They're saying it's a miracle."

"Oh my God," Jerry said again; a thin smile working its way across his face. "I am so happy for you."

"I haven't told Jim yet," she said. "I'm going to surprise him tonight."

"That is... That is amazing."

"Thank you so much Jerry, I'm so lucky to have you as my older brother." She paused. "Look, I just wanted you to be the first to hear it. I've gotta head to the store to grab some chicken and a bottle of wine for Jim and I. Let's grab lunch in the next day or so yeah?"

"Um, yeah," Jerry said. "That'd be nice.

"Ok Jer Bear. You have a good night OK?"

"Will do," he replied. "You too."

Beth hung up the phone, and Jerry brought his down from his ear, letting his hand drop to his side as he did. His eyes were locked onto the napkin in his open palm.

Inside the thin white paper were small chunks of tissue in the middle of a large bloodstain. The pieces of flesh were blackened along the edges, and smelled like rotted meat. He stared into the napkin as another urge to cough tickled its way up his throat, and the burning sensation in his chest continued to get worse.

He stared at the drying blood and cancerous tissue as his mind slowly blurred, and his breaths became short.

The last thing Jerry Aguilar saw before darkness fell over him, and gravity pulled his head to the couch cushion next to him, was his grandmothers toothless grin, and two pitch black voids where her eyes used to be.

SPIRIT WALK

"I had always thought that the 'good,' and the 'bad' and the 'violent' did not exist in any absolute, essential sense. It seemed to me interesting to demystify these adjectives in the setting of a Western. An assassin can display a sublime altruism while a good man can kill with total indifference."

-Sergio Leone-

Chapter 1

Rory Kyle sat on the painted horse, sweat pouring down his face, a glistening sheen of beaded moisture like a mask of wet fear, eyes narrow and red from the tears held back only from hatred. The rope around his neck was taught, a six-foot tether between his life, and the low hanging branch of the oak tree. Before him lay the bodies of his wife and children, butchered by the men that stood laughing before him.

"Your squaw didn't squeal like they usually do injun lover." The man speaking stood between him and the woman he had loved. "Matter a fact, I think she liked it."

Rory's insides burned, his stomach a steel knot in his gut. His jaw was clenched and he could taste blood in his mouth from where his teeth were pushing into his gums.

"I think his daughter liked it whole lot less though," the man standing near the well said, turning to drop the ladle down the hollow shaft and clicking his tongue against his cheek. "She did bleed though. Think she was fresh."

One of his teeth cracked.

Rory stared at the man, his eyes yearning to gaze the corpses of his family, but abhorrent hatred locking his gaze to the leader of the group, keeping them fixed on the man with the rolled cigarette in his hand, and his wife's shawl in the other.

The man brought the fabric up to his nose and inhaled deeply. "Think I'm gon' hang on to this for a while." He smiled. "Call it a keepsake; a little remembrance of our get together here."

The steel ball grew.

"See," the man continued, blowing his nose into the patterned cloth, and hocking up a spit, which he sent in the direction of Rory's wife. "If you'd a just seen things our way, and signed over the deed to your property like a civilized man, all this here coulda been avoided." He raised his arm out, panning from Rory's wife, to his children that lay scalped on the ground near her.

Rory took a shuddered breath, another tooth cracking in the back. He wanted to scream, wanted to tear the throats out of the men and hang them with their own windpipes; he wanted to tear the flesh from their bones, and drop them into a salt pile. Every evil he had never thought now flooded his mind.

"They didn't have to die today. You coulda lived the rest of your days, porkin' on that injun squaw and raising them little half-breed heathens." He threw the scarf at Rory and yelled, "But no!"

Rory felt the horse lurch at the outburst, and instinctively locked his legs tighter.

"You had to go making things difficult for us!"

The man stepped forward, his eyes narrowing, the other three men stepping closer. "And this is what you get, injun lover," the man said, his voice a low growl. "A dead wife, and two scalped kids, one still warm with my semen inside her."

Another tooth.

The man stepped forward and grabbed his leg. "Now, you rot in hell."

He slapped the horse and it lurched forward.

Rory felt himself slip from the blanket on its back and felt the noose tighten around his neck like a constrictor crushing its prey. His feet kicked wildly, grabbing desperately for the ground that was three feet below, his lungs burning with lurching breath unable to escape; then he heard three shots, and felt the bullets go deep into his chest.

The air was cool, and the breeze was light, blowing softly past his face. It felt good on the sweat. As his world faded to black, his thoughts went to the woman he loved, and the children they had raised together. He saw her sitting across from the fire from him those years ago, when he had arrived at the Apache camp; the beginning of the U.S. Army Ranger/Scout initiative. He could feel her bare skin against his, wrapped in the warmth of fur on their wedding night. He saw the birth of his daughter, and their son.

As his body twitched at the end of the braided rope, he felt release.

Chapter 2

Rory looked around him. The world was shrouded in mist, like an early morning fog enshrouding the surrounding woods. The air was still and unmoving, and he could feel not chill, nor warmth. He could see his breath in front of him, and as he stepped through the pale woods, he could hear the soft crunch of fallen leaves beneath his boots.

He walked in silence, when a sound caught his ear. It was ever so slight, but there was something familiar about it, something comforting, and inviting.

He walked through the trees towards the sound; a low rhythmic chanting that brought back old memories and stirred nervousness in his chest, but not that of apprehension.

He waded through the bluish grey, wooded haze, when the sound became clearer through the fog and he recognized what it was. It was an Apache song.

Rory had struggled at picking up tongue of his wife's people, and even after serving with them for five years, only knew a handful of words and phrases, but the language was undeniably distinct. He knew it well.

As he waded through the mist, pushing the occasional branch back, he walked in the direction of the familiar voice, an acoustic trail, drifting through the forest for him to follow.

He pushed a low hanging branch aside and stopped. Ahead of him, a knife's throw away was a coyote. It was small and thin and its wiry hair bristled in what Rory felt should be a chill that wasn't there. It stared at him for a moment and then turned quickly, trotting ten feet, and then stopping to glance back at him, and waited. Rory stared.

The coyote turned its head and glanced into the trees, and then back to him. It wanted him to follow.

Rory took a step towards it and it turned, heading in the direction of the chant. He tried to keep its pace in the hazy light, and every time he thought he had lost it, he would come to a spot and see it standing there waiting for him.

He followed the coyote for what felt like an eternity when he came to a clearing. He stepped into it and froze. The coyote was standing in front of his house.

How... How is this possible? I don't live in the

woods, and there's smoke coming from the chimney?

He stood there puzzled, when the coyote whined, and then ran off into the woods near the side of the house.

What is this? he thought to himself, stepping forward, taking step after step towards the structure he had built with his own hands many years ago.

As he approached the voice got louder, until it felt like it was all around him, enveloping him in a rhythmic hide.

He stepped to the door and reached out. As his hand neared he knob it opened, and began swinging inward with a deliberate slowness.

Rory stepped inside.

Sitting at the table in the main room were his children. His daughter Liluye and his son Brett smiled as he walked in, their food steaming with warmth in front of them. He felt his heart began to beat, slow at first, but its ferocity increasing.

As he stepped in, he saw his wife. She turned to him from the kitchen and smiled. His heart was beating heavy, the chanting sound loud in his ears, drowning everything else out, and then it stopped, and his wife whispered, "Go home."

Chapter 3

Rory's eyes shot open and he screamed. It was primal and long, the pain and agony of the loss of his family, and the death of everyone he loved, coming out in a long anguished cry.

As his eyes came to focus, he recognized the conical structure above him; he was in a tipi. It took a moment for it to click, and then he recognized the structure as the lodge he had spent hours in, learning to pray, and sweating in. It was the hut of Onawa's father.

He made an attempt to sit up, but as he did, strong hands rested on his shoulder, and a familiar voice spoke from beside him. "He says' you need rest. You are not yet ready to travel."

The voice came from an old friend, and fellow scout, Alchesay.

"How..?" Rory whispered. "I was dead."

The shaman spoke, followed by Alchesay. "He says that he has brought your spirit back to your body. It is heavy with vengeance, and cannot pass to the other side. Without bringing peace to your spirit, you would be stuck wandering the world between ours, and our

129

ancestors forever. You must make right what was done, you must exact justice on those that have done this to you; and to his daughter, and grandchildren." The old man continued to speak. "As long as those who have done this live, you will be made to walk this earth. You are not alive, and you are not dead, but in between, as your spirit is. Once you have killed the men, and brought rest to your spirit, then it will be free to walk to the other side, and join your family."

Rory's throat was dry, and as he attempted to speak, he heard his friend whisper, "Shhhh. You must take time. You are weak. You must get strong. You will need to for the battle ahead."

He let his head fall back into the fur behind it, and the smell of sage and spice filled his nose as the point above him faded into the distance, and sleep pulled him away.

Chapter 4

Rory wandered in the dream world, his surroundings changing and shifting with his memories. He was surrounded by the fields of his childhood; watching the river behind the house he grew up in flow by slowly, his father at his side smiling. He could see the smoke from the Apache tribe rising up in the distance; messages being sent on the wind. He heard laughter from his sister, and felt the loving presence of his mother. Then the skies began to darken, storm clouds growing ominously overhead. He heard the low rolling rumble of thunder, followed by the sharp, deafening clap of lightning. Something was wrong.

Rory rose from his spot on the bank, and as he turned, heard the screams; his wife's. "Onawa!" he shouted, picking up his pace towards his house.

Another clap.

He pushed himself to run, his arms trying desperately to swim through the thick, liquid air, trying to propel himself faster towards his house, and the shrieks of his wife.

As he got closer he saw the painted horse. It

stood just off to his house, tethered by a thick rope to the oak tree at the edge of his yard. It turned to him, eyes black as coals and pawed heavily at the ground. There was blood seeping from the top of its hooves, and its mouth frothed heavy with congealed saliva. It neighed loudly and reared up as he made his way past, and he could see that the rope wrapped around its neck, and that the noose was getting tighter.

He passed the unholy visage, and pushed his way up the stairs, swimming through the congealed air towards his front door.

When he reached the top he grabbed the knob and swung the door inwards. All sound stopped, and the swirling clouds above froze in place.

Rory looked through the door at his front yard. He turned and saw his empty house behind him.

He slowly made his way out onto the porch, and looked around. The horse was gone, and the sky had settled into a dull grey, the massive storm all but dissipated, leaving a sky void of color, and an air deathly quiet.

He looked to the road leading away from his house, and saw his wife lying off to the side, his children lined up next to her. He rushed towards them.

As he approached he stopped, seeing the face of his beloved, battered and bruised, the glistening white behind liquid red of his children's skulls where they had been scalped; his oldest daughters dress torn upwards, a thin spatter of blood between her thighs.

He dropped to the ground, his knees landing heavy in the dirt and cried. He sat there sobbing, his face in his hands, pressing into his eyes to block out the vision before him, when he felt a hand touch his shoulder.

He stopped; letting his hands fall slowly downwards, and realized he was in the hut. He turned his head and looked up to see his wife standing over him, her face solemn and forgiving. "I'm so sorry," he said, reaching up to take her hand. "I'm so sorry I couldn't stop them."

She looked at him lovingly, and without moving her lips, spoke. "We're waiting for you Rory. You have to make this right."

"I will," he said, a shake in his voice all that held back the reservoir of tears and anguish. "I swear."

"Make this right," she said, softly pulling her

hand away and stepping backwards.

"Please," he begged, pleading for her not to go with that single word.

"Make this right."

Rory shuddered, watching his wife fade into the darkness. His eyes fell to the dirt in front of him, and all anguish disappeared. He felt anger filling his soul, hatred and malice flooding into him. His hands balled into fists at his side, and the stinging lines of salt running down his cheeks fueled it even deeper. There was no more sadness, no more tears. There was only one thing left; revenge.

Chapter 5

Rory awoke to the sound of a crow cawing in the distance. The warm morning air grazed over the thin layer of sweat that covered him in a soft mist.

He brought himself upright and moved his hand to his chest, to the spot the bullets had entered. He ran his fingers over the scars, took a deep breath and then filling his lungs with the smell of sage and cured buffalo hide.

He stood, his legs giving little shake to his weight, walked to the pile of clothes folded neatly near the entrance, and dressed.

As he folded the flap to the lodge back the sun washed over him, caressing his body with a warmth he had all but forgotten inside the tipi. He could feel his feet connecting to the earth, but not like before. It was as if every step he took, his feet molded with it, becoming part of the soil beneath him, and stretching to snap with every lift.

He made his way to the center of the camp to find many of the villagers sitting around a large fire pit full of smoldering ash.

As he approached he saw the Chief; the Shaman at his side, and his friend across from them. He walked up, and the Shaman nodded to him, and then held his hand out in the direction of the chief.

His eyes moved slowly to the Chief who pulled his gaze from the ring of stones, and slowly reached forward, lifting a piece of cloth from an object in front of him. It was a tomahawk. He spoke, and his friend translated from across the pit. "Men have taken from you, what was not theirs to take. These men are not deserving to walk this earth. It is you that will send them to the next world, to a world that will reflect their deeds on this one. You must return home, and bury your wife and children, for they cannot rest until you have." The chief reached down and picked up the tomahawk, lifting it up to Rory. "The shaman has guided your spirit back to your body, but only so your physical form and make ready your spirits journey to the next world, where you may once again, rejoin your family. Know this Gotál; you are neither alive, nor dead. Your spirit will not rest until you have avenged your family. When your task is completed, then, and only then, may you travel to the other side."

Rory took the tomahawk, and slid it into his belt. "Ahee-ih-yeh," he said, thanking the Chief, and then repeating to the Shaman. "Thank you," he said to his friend, and then turned to leave camp.

As he was approaching the edge, a woman came towards him, leading a horse. She held the reigns out and lowered her head.

He rubbed the long face of the creature, and then swung himself atop its back and made his way out of the camp towards his house.

It was less than a half-day later when he saw the life he once knew at the end of the road he followed.

Chapter 6

Rory slowed the horse to a walk as he approached his house, and steeled himself for what he was to endure; the burying of his family.

He saw their bodies lying on the side of the road where he had died; disfigured and bloated.

He lowered himself from his horse, and tied it loosely to the fence that ran the edge of his property, and made his way to them. He stopped, the feeling in his chest nearly bursting, and his breath coming in short, staggered gasps.

He turned and made his way to the small barn out back, and retrieved a shovel. He then made his way to his backyard and begun to dig.

Hours later there were three holes in the ground. He took blankets from inside his house, and wrapped a bandana around his face to cover the smell, and made his way to the road, wrapping each of them up and carrying them carefully to the back, where he lay them gently into their resting places, and covered them with earth.

He fashioned three crosses from pieces of wood

cut from the tree he was hung from, placed them at the heads of their graves, and then made his way back into the house.

He entered the bedroom he had slept the last fifteen years in, and slid the bed his wife and he had shared aside. He then took the tomahawk from his belt, and pried up one of the floorboards, setting it aside, and then ripping up three more.

Minutes passes as he stared down into the space that had been covered by the boards, and after some time, he took a deep breath, exhaled, and then leaned forward, pulling a small wooden crate from below.

He set the crate on the bed, and slowly opened the lid. Folded neatly inside was his ranger's uniform, his army issued pistol belt and rifle, and a fair amount of ammunition for both.

He slowly removed his clothing, and then with delicate, practiced precision, put his uniform on, wrapping his gun belt around his waist, and picking the loaded rifle up.

He grabbed his bow and quiver from above the door and made his way outside, and walked to where his wife's sash had blown into a bush a ways off, and pulled it free. He brought it to his face and inhaled deeply, breathing in the smell of her skin, and hearing the faint sound of her laughter as he did. He then tied it around his waist, and made his way back to her.

As he stood in front of their graves, he fought for the words to say.

He kneeled and closed his eyes, bringing their image to his mind clearly and spoke. "I swear to you, that those who have done this to you will pay. I will kill every single man that had anything to do with this. I will not rest, until I have sent every one of them to hell." He opened his eyes, which now burned with the heat of fire, hatred flowing wildly behind them and stood. He turned, making his way to the horse in front, and climbed atop. He knew where he was heading; a small encampment just in the hills to the south. He had heard whispering when in town about a small camp that a local gang had been using, coming down every now and then to raid camps, and raise hell in town. This is where he would head, and this is where he would find out who had done this to him.

Chapter 7

The sun was already beginning to drop below the horizon when he entered the canyon. He could hear the distant howls of coyotes, and saw a hawk circling overhead.

He scanned the canyon walls for scouts, but there were none; they probably didn't think anyone was stupid enough to come looking for them.

Rory tied the horse up at the bottom and pulled his rifle from the sling he'd attached to the back of the saddle. He checked his pistol and started his way inwards.

He could tell by the tracks that they had returned to camp earlier that afternoon, and that no one had come or gone since. *Good*, he thought, that meant they were still there.

As he made his way inwards he began to catch whiff of a campfire. He could smell coffee, and buffalo meat cooking. They had already begun to settle down for dinner. *That's good*, he thought, *that means they won't be on guard.*

He made his way up the side of the canyon,

climbing the steep wall to the ridge above, and silently made his way further, till he could see the camp below. He counted; four men, five horses. That meant one of them wasn't in the camp. *Probably watching the entrance*, he thought.

He stared down at them for a short while, watching their movements, hatred sloshing inside his gut as he heard them laugh and share stories.

He slid slowly backwards down the ridge, making his way back down to the trail that lead to the camp, and took his boots off. He had learned from the Apache, that when you go into battle, and you need to not be noticed, you removed your boots and allowed the earth to carry your steps with silence.

He rounded a corner and saw the man that went with the extra horse. He was sitting at the entrance to a makeshift gate that led to the encampment.

Rory paused, slinking back behind the rock he was crouching behind.

He needed to get past the man, and without being heard. This attack needed to be by surprise, and he needed to ensure that at least one of them was left alive.

He took a deep breath and then reached down, picking up a fist sized stone, and lobbing it down the trail. It landed heavy, bouncing off of a boulder and rolling a little ways down.

Rory waited.

He could smell tobacco smoke getting closer before he heard the shuffle of boots, and then moments later the barrel of a rifle came past the boulder, the man immediately after.

Rory stood, and silently made his way behind the man, pulling his knife from his belt as he did.

He followed his steps, matching them perfectly with his own to further silence his presence.

When they were safely out of earshot from the camp he stepped forward, grabbed the man's forehead, and pulled back, the edge of his blade opening a valley through his windpipe and jugular.

He brought his foot against the back of the man's knee, and brought him quietly to the ground. He waited for the gurgling gasps; the sound of a man drowning in lung full's of his own blood, to stop, and then drug him off the path.

He snapped a sagebrush at its base and used it to sweep dirt across the spreading pool of blood; no need for anyone to find out sooner that he was there if they came back. Then he made his way upwards.

As he passed the gate he reached into his pack and pulled an apple out, slicing it in half with his knife. He then took one half and squeezed the juice out, and spread it across his arms and chest. He wanted to make sure that he was welcome by the men's horses as he made his way past, and that they didn't startle as he approached.

He walked up the path, and slowly approached their horses, giving them each a small piece of the remaining apple, and untying their ropes as they softly munched. He then snuck in behind that chuck wagon they were behind.

The campfire cast eerie shadows underneath the wagon in the fading light as Rory ducked behind one of the wheels to look underneath it. He could see the four men sitting around the fire.

He waited.

Rory knew it would only be a matter of time until one of them needed to get up, and he needed to make sure that none of them was facing him as he entered, so he stayed kneeling, listening to their conversation as he did. None of these men were the ones from his house, this he knew. He had memorized their voices well, had dreamt them, and heard them over and over, whenever his mind became still. He would recognize them, and remembered them well.

As he sat there, his mind wandered back to Onawa, and when he had first laid eyes on the woman he knew he was destined to spend his life with.

* * *

Rory had been a decorated officer in the United States Army. He had been at the lead of a Ranger division stationed in Arizona. He had been chosen to take part in a secret military plan, which would bring the best Rangers the Army had, with the best scouts the Apache had to form the United States Army Indian Scout division. This is how he came to meet his wife.

Rory had been sent to an Apache camp to meet with their Chief. The night he arrived, he was sitting near the fire, passing the pipe with the others, when Onawa brought food. His gaze locked with hers, and instantly he knew she was the one.

During the course of the next year and a half, he lived between the camp, and his base. He learned to fight and hunt like the Apache, and acted as the go between with the Army commanders, and the Apache Chief, who also led the Native Council.

When his duties were coming to an end, he asked the Chief for Onawa's hand in marriage. He went through a ceremony, and by binding blood with Alchesay, became a member of the tribe, and was named Gotál; Coyote in the Apache tongue. Rory was granted permission to marry, and they held the ceremony that night.

They had set up a homestead a day's ride from the Apache camp, so she could remain close to her ancestors, and her family, and they began their life together. It was less than a year later that their first child, Liluye was born, a year later their son; Brett.

They had lived peacefully, Rory remaining a scout, and working with the Army from time to time, and his wife raising the children. That was until the men arrived, and told him that he needed to sell his land. That was when everything went bad.

* * *

Rory sat, listening to them talk, when his opportunity came. One of the men stood up and said, "I'm unna take a leak, damn pisswater runnin right through me."

He leaned back, looking between the wagons spokes and saw the man facing him get up and make his way to the edge of camp. That's when he took a deep breath, pulled his pistol and stepped out from behind the wagon.

There were four flashes; three from his pistol, and one from the eyes of the man that had walked to the edge of the firelight to piss.

Two of the men by the fire slumped over, bullet holes passing through the back of their skulls to the jumping flames, the other stared at Rory for a moment, eyes slowly crossing to look for the trickle of blood now running down his face. Then he dropped.

The man that had walked away spun, pants dropping around his ankles, a stream of urine still flowing, and before he could level his pistol, Rory threw his knife quick and accurate, punching a hole in the man's wrist causing the pistol to fly aside.

Rory walked towards him past the others that

lie dead, the one on his right now lay face-first in the fire, sending the acrid smell of burning hair and flesh into the air.

"Please mister," the man standing with the dropped trousers said as he approached. "We ain't done nothing'."

Rory walked past the fire.

"I can't feel my hand..." the man continued.

Rory pulled the tomahawk from his belt.

"Oh come on mister, please," the man begged, trying to step backwards.

"The Kyle homestead," Rory said, his words coming out as a grumbled hiss. "Who!?" he yelled.

"Who what mister?" the man replied, his knees starting to shake.

"Who killed them?" Rory asked, his voice lowering again, his knuckles past the point of white on the leather-wrapped handle.

"I don't know mister," the man replied, his eyes shooting to his dead friends, one of them now burning. "Honest."

Rory flipped the blade outwards in a flash, and stepped forward at the same time, bringing the cold metal against the side of the man's genitals. "Who was it!!!" he yelled.

"OK, OK!! The man yelled, "I'll tell you! Fuck!"

"Now." Rory growled.

"It was Bill Harding. Bill Harding was the one; him and his boys. There's four of em. They holed up in the saloon in Coral City. If they're not out doing work for the mayor, they're at the saloon. I swear. Please."

Bill Harding. He had heard that name before; like the whisper of snake moving across the sand.

Rory put the tomahawk back in his belt and turned around. He made it four paces when the man spoke up. "They're gon' kill you, you know that right?"

Rory stopped and turned around. "They already did," he replied with a squint in his eyes. Then he brought his pistol up and shot the man in the face.

He watched the man's head explode across the rocks behind him and slowly let his revolver lower. Then he turned around walked back down the canyon.

It was a three-hour ride to Coral City, which would put him there at just around two. No one would expect anything that late. Nobody knew the hell that was coming for them.

Chapter 8

On the way to Coral City, Rory stopped back at his house for the last time.

He tied up his horse, took a lantern from the front gate and lit it, and then made his way to his wife's grave at the back.

He walked up and took his hat off, letting it drop to his side, and kneeled once more in front of her grave, setting the lantern behind him.

"I have found them," he spoke. "I know now, who it was that did this. I know you would not want me to do the things that I am about to do, and I can only hope for your forgiveness, but these men are evil. They have done wicked things, not only to us, but others, and if I don't do this, they will continue to do these things again and again. I know, if you were here right now, you'd tell me to put this behind me, and to try and carry on with my life, but I can't. I can't live, thinking they have done the things they did, to you, and Liluye. I am stuck here until this is finished, halfway between life and death, and the only way for me to ever be with you again, is to do the things you would want me not to. For this I am sorry my love. Please forgive me, and watch over the children until I can join you."

He pulled his knife from his belt, and brought the blade to his face, cutting a thin line across each cheek. The then stabbed the blade into the earth and mixed the dripping blood into the soil, and with it, painted three large striped across his cheeks. He then pulled the blade from the earth, slid it into his belt, grabbed his hat and stood. He stared at his family's graves, the stinging pulsing across his cheeks, and put his hat on. "I'll be joining you soon," he whispered, tearing his eyes away from the mounds and turning in the direction of his horse, picking up the lantern as he left.

As he passed his house, he paused, and then threw the lantern into the open doorway and watched as the kerosene splashed across the floor he had built, and turned the house into an inferno.

He stood there for a moment, watching the blaze get larger, and then turned and walked to his horse.

Death was coming, and by the end of this night, there would be a lot less room in Hell.

Chapter 9

By the time Rory reached the outskirts of Coral City, the moon was at its nighttime peak; bright and full in a cloudless sky. The air had a chill that Rory didn't notice, the kind only desert animals felt as they scurried into their night nests, or stalked their prey in the dark.

He stopped a short walk from the edge of town and tied his horse to a lonesome tree, unpacking his rifle, and tying it to the side of his saddle in case he needed it during a quick exit. Then he turned and started towards the lights.

As he approached the edge of town he formulated his plan, and when he saw a trade wagon at the beginning of the main street, everything fell into place.

He walked towards the wagon, taking mental note of the layout he had seen hundreds of times before when hitting the supply store, or the occasional stop at the barber for a shave, or his yearly poker night at the saloon.

He made his way to the back of the wagon and pulled a match from his pocket, striking it against the wheel and lighting up the fabric cover. Then he made his way around the wagon, and quickly darted across the street to sneak between buildings until he was on the side of the saloon, and then waited.

It was a few minutes until the wagon had fully caught fire, and the smell of smoke had garnered the attention of a late night patron staggering their way out of the saloon. "Fire!" he heard the man yell, followed by the sound of men rushing outside to see.

He waited until they were all busy, rushing to put out the fire, or just be there to talk about it after. That's when he made his way into the saloon.

Rory pushed the swinging doors open and stepped inside. The air was stale with old cigar smoke and cheap whiskey. The bartender was polishing glasses behind the bar, and the only patrons left inside were the four men preoccupied by their poker game at the table; none willing to walk away from their earnings.

As he stepped in one of the men at the table looked up, and Rory said a single name; "Bill Harding."

The man looking up made eye contact with one of the other men at the table, and Rory knew without asking they knew who he was asking about.

The man at the table looked at him, and his eyes turned to a squint. "Who's askin'?"

"Where is he?" Rory responded, his hand moving comfortably close to the handle of his pistol.

The man threw another exchanged glance, and the man in the exchange slowly turned to see who was speaking. When he did, a look of recognition crossed his face, and his features slackened. He whispered, "It can't be..." and held his gaze on Rory.

"Where is he?" Rory repeated.

The man facing him stood, two of the others at the table taking his lead, and turning to face him.

Rory didn't wait. Before the men could react, before they could even fathom what was happening, Rory had drawn his pistol, and was palming the hammer, throwing lead faster than the sounds could be distinguished between.

Three of the men dropped instantly, the fourth spinning from the molten lead that became lodged in his shoulder.

Rory saw the barkeep reach under the counter, and recognized the look of murder in his face, and put his fifth round between his eyes, a rooster tail of blood and brain painting the mirror behind him. Then he walked up to the man on the floor and repeated himself. "Where is Bill Harding?"

The man coughed. "I don't know." He reached for his shoulder with his other hand. "Curtis. He knows. I just hired on. I swear."

Rory stared at him, and cocked the hammer of his revolver back, when movement on the stairs caught his eye, and he saw another man making his way down from above. He pulled his tomahawk, and with practiced skill sent it twirling end over end across the room, plunging its sharp edge deep into the man's chest, sending him dropping to the stairs, and sliding the rest of the way down. Then he pointed the pistol at the man on the floors face and pulled the trigger.

He walked towards the stairs, pausing to pull his tomahawk from the dead man's chest with a wet *thwuck*, and wiped the blade on the man's vest, then put it back into his belt and reloaded his gun. Then he made his way up the stairs.

When he reached the top he saw that there were six rooms along the hall. He decided to work his way down.

He approached the first door and hugged the wall, grabbing the handle, and swinging the door open. As he looked in he saw one of the saloon's whores riding on top of one of the men. Her hips were moving in a circular motion, and the man's hands were grasped onto her thighs, his fingers holding tight to her flesh. Rory stepped in.

"What the!?" the man yelled, throwing the whore aside, landing her heavy on the floor next to the bed with a thud. He lunged for his pistol belt at the foot of the bed, and Rory unloaded two rounds into him; one in the side to slow him down, and one in the side of the head for good measure. Then he turned and made his way into the hallway.

The gunfight had gotten the attention of the other men in the hall, and one of the doors flew open, a man stepping out with his pistol leveled. Rory ducked back in the room as three bullets planted into the wooden frame near his head.

He took his hat off and tossed it into the hall.

Three more shots. Then he stepped out and put a bullet into the man's throat.

He made his way to the next door and tried the

handle; locked. He stood a little off to the side, and kicked it in. Huddled behind the bed were two whores, one naked, and the other very close to being so as well. He turned and made his way back out.

The next door was unlocked; the room empty, so he tried the second to last.

As he approached the door he paused, and then hugged the wall again, and tapped on the door with the barrel of his pistol. Four shots blasted out from the door, sending a shower of splinters into the hall. Rory took aim and shot the handle of the door, sending the brass pieces skipping across the floor, and the door swinging slightly inwards. Another two shots.

Rory kicked the door inwards with his heel, and then spun around the edge, drawing his pistol on a man that stood there with both hands raised in the air. "Curtis?" Rory asked with a growl.

The man pointed his finger to the room across the hall.

Rory nodded, and turned, making his way out, and then as he reached the doorway, pointed his pistol behind him and sent another soul to the devil.

He made his way across the hall, and tapped on

the door. "I know you're in there Curtis." Rory yelled at the door. A three-bullet answer responded to him through the door.

Rory repeated his actions, shooting the handle to the door, sending it opening the slightest, another two shots in return.

Rory slowly sunk down the wall, lying on his side next to the wall and pushed the door open with his gun. Two more shots. Either the man had reloaded, or had more than one pistol.

Rory could see from his vantage point, the man's legs behind the bed in the room, and took aim at his ankles, releasing four shots that brought the man to a heap at his level. He then brought himself to his feet and made his way into the room, quickly rounding the edge of the bed, and putting a bullet into Cutis's shoulder to keep him from trying for the gun that had fallen from his grasp when his ankles exploded.

"Where's Bill Harding?" Rory shouted, his pistol aimed at the man's forehead.

"Fuck you," the man spat.

Rory lowered the pistol to the man's crotch and repeated himself. "Where, is Bill Harding?"

The man could see in his eyes that he was not there to play games, and that the gun aimed at his crotch was much more than just an idle threat; his interrogator meant business. "Look, He's at the Mayor's place outside of town. Him and the rest of the Hideaway Gang are holed up in there somethin fierce. They're the Mayors personal bodyguards."

"The Mayor?" Rory asked, puzzled from not hearing that Coral City had elected someone to fill that role.

"Yeah, George Whitley. He kinda became the unofficial mayor of Coral City when he hired the Hideaway's to start enforcin' for him. Anyone that opposed his newfound title was made dead. Now he pretty much runs the town. Anything that happens, well, it goes through him. Word is, he's tryin' to expand his horizons as well; been buyin up all kinds a land, making some deal with the railroad or something, working on makin' this town a regular stop along the path. He's takin' out anyone who stands against him, or doesn't wanna sell."

Rory stayed quiet, the hammer of his pistol slowly cocking back.

"That's all I know!" the man said, fear building up like a growing wave behind his eyes. "I swear."

"How many are there?" Rory asked.

"I don't know; twenty, maybe more. Been a month since I been out there, he coulda recruited more."

Rory nodded, his gaze falling to the floor for a moment, and then back up to the man. "I was a good man once," he said. "But it was men like you that changed me." He paused again. "I hope it's hot as they say it is down there."

Rory turned and made his way out of the room, the barrel of his pistol still smoking as he holstered it and made his way down the stairs. As he exited the saloon he could see the men at the end of the street just managing to get the burning wagon under control. When the ammunition crate on it had started going off, it had put the firefight on hold for a few minutes, and covered the battle raging in the saloon.

Rory walked past the men without a word, and disappeared into the blanket of night. He was a twenty-minute ride from the self-appointed mayor's house. He had another five hours to get ready for the war that was about to take place, and he was approaching this with a different tactic; fighting the Apache way.

Chapter 10

When Rory arrived at the ranch house, he took his rifle, bow and quiver, and bag with guns collected while leaving the saloon from the men he had killed, and made his way to the edge of the property. It was still dark, and he used the cover of night to sneak around the edges, placing the weapons behind small hills in different places, covering them with small pieces of brush. His plan was to wait for the sun to just crest over the horizon, and start his battle with the sun at his back, and sleep still in the eyes of his enemies. He would run from spot to spot, staying only long enough to take out one or two men, and then making his way to the next. He wanted to confuse the men, and hopefully make them believe they were under attack by a group, not one man; that way they wouldn't be so quick to rush out and attack, giving him more time to pick them off one by one. He also knew the advantage of having the sun at his back, and the fact that most of the men would be rushing into battle still half asleep, their senses dulled, and their awareness at its lowest. He would exploit these weaknesses, and use them to hopefully kill most of them before making his way into the house. This was all dependent upon things working out as he planned, but lucky for him, this wasn't the first time in his life he had planned an ambush like this. This was however, the first time he had done it with hatred and revenge being the motivating factor, and not orders from above.

He spent the next two hours slowly making his way from spot to spot, digging small trenches in which he could lie in long enough to attack without being seen or shot, and walked the perimeter a few times to get a mental layout of the structure. He didn't want any surprises as he rushed in; like miscalculating the amount of men inside, from which he could gather was twenty three by the count of horses in the stable behind the house.

He made his way back to the front of the house, and settled himself down into one of the makeshift trenches and waited. He had another few hours until the sun rose as his ally; another few hours to let the hatred build, and another few hours to make peace with himself.

Chapter 11

When the sun had begun to crest the horizon, Rory watched the first few rays pierce the yellowing skies, and then rolled over onto his stomach to gaze upon the house. There were two men in front, lazily walking out to do their morning piss routines. Rory took a deep breath and grasped the bow lying next to him in his hands, and waited for the men to part company. The moment they were out of each other's presence, he rose to his knee, and let the first arrow fly. It landed its target, piercing the first man's neck, cutting off any scream that might come forth. By the time he had hit the ground, a second arrow was already slicing the air, honing in on the back of the second man's skull.

Rory waited. He was running out of time. The morning's glare was the brightest, and his window only lasted about twenty minutes.

He leaned down and grabbed one of the arrows he had wrapped tightly with cloth at the tip. He had dipped the arrow in a kerosene can he had come across while checking the perimeter earlier that evening, in preparation for the flight it was about to take.

He pulled a match out of his pocket, and struck it against a small rock, bringing the tip to life with a quick flash; then he touched it to the cloth and ignited the tip of the arrow.

He loaded it against the string of the bow and took aim at an open window in the front of the house, took a breath and held, and then let the arrow fly. It struck its target. Now all he had to do was wait.

A few minutes went by, and the moment he heard the first yell, he struck a match, lit his second arrow, and let it fly into the stables to the side of the house. He had already untethered the horses and left their pens open. The flames would ensure they would be countryside within moments, leaving no quick escape for those inside.

One of the men came running out of the house with a pail, charging in the direction of the well. His sprint fell short twenty feet from the front porch with an arrow through his side. Moments later another man exited. This time, Rory waited until he saw his friend and stopped.

Another in the neck.

Rory estimated that he would have already had

to move positions, but as long as they kept coming out single file, he would stay there and pick em off as they came. It was another five men before one stopped at the doorway and saw the bodies of the others and yelled something into the house; his yell was cut short by an Apache arrow, and that's when the gunshots began.

Rory saw as two of the windows in the house were broken out from the inside, and shots were being fired at random. As long as the bullets flew without target, that meant they had no idea where he was. He waited until one of the men held his head in the window long enough to get a shiny new hole through his forehead before he moved to the next spot.

Rory had taken up a spot off to the side of the front porch, and watched as round after round of ammunition blasted away at the small hill he had been behind, and the hat that was sitting on a rock there. Eventually the bullets stopped, and two men made their way out onto the porch. Rory smiled.

Rory was up already sprinting around the backside of the house, flanking to the other side of the porch before the second man had even hit the ground.

Moments later he was sitting across the other side, watching as men fired on the spot he just left. He knew it was only a matter of time until whoever was in charge ordered another two souls to be delivered to Satan. Less than two minutes. Ten left.

Rory made it back to the bow, and his hat.

He grabbed the bow and locked an arrow into place, waiting for his next shot, which came in the form of someone trying to sneak past the open door. Another clean shot.

Rory darted to the spot he was before, and then crept around to the back of the house. He could hear yelling, and heard someone say something about an Apache attack. His plan had worked like a charm. He loaded his last cloth tipped arrow, and sent it into a back window. Then he made his way back around and waited.

After a few moments he heard more gunshots; men shooting at an empty hill from the back of the house. He decided it was time to head inside.

Rory decided to enter the house from the left side. He crept past a window and took a look inside through a small space in the curtains. He could see five men huddled, talking frantically amongst themselves. The fire was still burning, and there was two men trying to put it out with blankets. The house was filling with smoke. He snuck around the edge, walking low and steady, a trick learned by the Apache for this exact purpose; to walk beneath windowsills and fences without being seen. He checked his revolver, and loaded two shells in; full rounds. As he approached the front door he stopped, pausing to take a deep breath, and the dove sideways into the doorway, sliding across the floor on his side, palming the hammer of his Colt at the same time, dropping the five men in the group in a flash, and then sent his knife spinning through the air at one of the men that was dropping a blanket they were holding.

He sat up instantly and rolled backwards out of the house back onto the porch, five bullets tearing up the floorboards where he had just lay.

He swung backwards against the outside wall and immediately reloaded, sneaking back to the window he had looked through to get a bead on the other man. As he did, a bullet shattered the glass, sending a rain of shards down on him. He stuck his hand

168

over the sill and fired three shots without looking, and then darted to the back of the house.

The back room he had launched the arrow into was now in flames. He paused long enough to reload, and then bolted around the other side of the house, and returned to the doorway. As he peered inside, he saw the other man with his back to him, looking out the other window. Rory stood and calmly raised his pistol, putting a bullet in the back of the man's head, and made his way inside. Two men left by his count.

He headed towards the stairs, and just as he was about to reach them, a man stepped out from behind a curtain at the top with his pistol drawn and fired. Rory took a punch to the gut as a molten piece of lead plunged its way into his stomach, lodging somewhere near his spine. He could feel the flesh searing inside, and brought his hand down to the hole. He looked up, and as he saw a smile start to build on the gunman's face, pulled his tomahawk and launched it up the stairs in the blink of an eye, slamming the man full force in the shoulder with the honed edge, sending him spinning against the wall behind him, and the gun in his hand flying sideways.

169

Rory was up the stairs in four bounds, standing over the man in moments.

"Who are you?" the man growled.

Rory recognized the man. He was the one that had stood there watching as his family was tortured and killed. He was the one that had slapped the horse. He was the one that was responsible; he had killed him.

"Bill Harding." Rory hissed.

"Wait a minute," the man began. "I recognize you."

Rory slowly lifted his pistol.

"It can't be," the man said, a look of fear working its way in behind his eyes. "We killed you. I killed you myself. Ain't nobody gets hung and shot, and lives.

Rory aimed the barrel of the pistol at the man's crotch. "You took everything from me." He hissed through clenched teeth. "You took my wife. You took my children. You took my house, and my property, and you took my life."

Rory cocked the hammer of the pistol back.

"Hold up," Bill began. "I was just under orders. It was the Mayor that was responsible for all this. I's just doin' what I's told."

"Funny," Rory said. "That's exactly what I'm doing."

He pulled the trigger, blasting the front of Bill's pants open, and reducing his personal works into nothing more than thin strips of tattered flesh protruding from a bloody denim opening.

Bill screamed.

"I want you to feel this," Rory yelled. "I want you to live in this moment forever." He reached down, grabbed Bils other arm and brought his tomahawk down on it hard, severing the arm at the wrist, the twitching hand falling to the floor next to the mangled genitals. Harding screamed, the sounds of a dying animal coming from his throat.

Rory reached up and cut a cord from the curtain and tied Bill's legs together at the ankles, and then reached up and slapped him in the face as he started to drift off into shock.

"You stay awake!" Rory yelled. "You don't get to die that easy.

The fire had spread, and the heat and smoke was intense. Rory could feel his back saturated in sweat from the heat of the blaze below as he turned to make his way to the Mayor's office.

He got to the door at the end of the hall and kicked it in. The mayor was cowering behind a very expensive looking chair, behind an even more expensive desk.

"Look," the Mayor began. "Whatever you want, take it; it's yours."

"I already have," Rory said. "I've taken everything that means anything to you. I've killed every single one of your men, I have taken everything that could be of any worth to whatever family you may have. I've taken Coral City from you, and now I'm going to take what you took from me; your life."

"I, I … I don't even know who you are mister," the Mayor pleaded. "Whatever I've done to do you wrong, well I apologize about that. My men have a way of doing things on their own without being told. I can't be held responsible for everything they do, I mean, they are grown men, and grown men, well, they do what they want."

Rory stood there listening to the fat man's sniveling, feeling the toxins released from his pierced stomach working their way through his insides, and his pulse beginning to slow from blood loss.

"My name is Rory Kyle," he said, walking towards the Mayor, pulling his knife as he did. "I want you to know, as you die, I did this to you. This is your last moment on this earth, and no, this won't release you. We both know where you're headed, but this will allow my spirit free."

He reached out and stuck the knife into the Mayor's throat, watching as his pupils dilated, and he gasped, choking on the steel beneath his Adam's apple.

Rory twisted the blade and let go, staggering backwards and hitting the floor.

As his eyes rose to the ceiling, he felt the last of his life leaving his body, and the ceiling began to get farther and farther away, until there was nothing left but black.

Chapter 12

The sky was a cloudy blue, light cotton tufts floating slowly against an azure background. The fields were a bloom of flowers, far as the eye could see. Rory could smell the lavender and honeysuckle wafting on the breeze, and the smell of pine drifting in from the distance with fresh brook water laced behind it.

As he walked through the field he could see his house growing closer with each step. When he was close enough to make out the curtains his wife had sewn in the window, a warmth began to fill his heart. He smiled as he saw thin smoke drifting upwards from the top of the chimney, caught in the lazy breeze.

He drifted slowly towards his home, and saw the door slowly begin to open. His heart fluttered, and he could feel tears beginning to form along the bottom of his eyelids.

"Onawa," he whispered as his wife stepped onto the porch, her tan leather caressing her frame, this tassels drifting in the breeze along her sleeves, and bottom of her dress. Her black hair was tied into two long braids, and the turquoise around her neck seemed

174

to shimmer in the light, reflecting the clear sky above.

He walked towards her, and saw her smile, stepping aside so his children could emerge from the house.

Elation washed over him, and he felt his breath wash away as he heard his son yell, "Pa!!" and dart towards him, his daughter running softly behind.

The world around him bloomed as the memories of his life before, and his anger faded away, replaced by the loving embrace of his family. He was now where he belonged; he was home.

THE
LIST

"The LORD has made himself known; he has executed judgment; the wicked are snared in the work of their own hands."

-Psalms 9:16-

The air in the cabin was stale, the musky odor of old pine and termite riddled rafters hung in the air like a worn out air freshener in a derelict junkyard car. The light from the candles threw flickers of shadows across the walls, which fluttered through the exposed beams overhead like flames licking the flue of an oversized fireplace.

Seated in the middle of the dim room was man in his early twenties. His hair was well kempt, and an air of Abercrombie wafted from the red Hollister polo that fit his sweat covered athletic build.

"Please. Please. Tell me what I did!!"

The words fell forth from the affluent lips of the distressed soul, an accent wavering between Calabasas and Brentwood bringing a trickle of contempt to the stomach of the man standing near a table to his left.

"I didn't do anything, please."

The sobs fell on unempathetic ears as the man at the table laid out a foray of small instruments that looked as if he was about to do surgery on a tiny robot. There were clips and wires, small gadgets with hooks and screws, and a small assortment of surgical blades and clamps.

The man at the table was placing everything in an order with unblinking, methodical movements.

"My parents have money; I can get you anything you want, please! Please."

The man at the table turned around and stepped towards the other who instinctively cringed away. As the captor loomed over him he raised the candle in his hand. Light moved past the armrests of the crude wooden chair. The younger man's arms were secured to the thick planks with half-inch diameter bolts that pierced directly through the wood, flesh and bone. There was blood pooled around the base of the chair, and light danced off the thin wire securing the captives ankles to the legs of the structure.

The older gentleman looked closely into the face of the struggling prisoner, the candlelight glinting off his grey hair as he leaned down and then turned to make his way back to the table.

"You motherFUCKER!" the man yelled at his captor's back. "I'll fucking kill you..."

"Joshua Tree," the older man said, his eyes locked to the table before him.

"What..?" the man bound in the chair

whispered. "What are you talking about? God..."

"No Caleb," the man holding the page said. "God has nothing to do with this, he turned his back on you in that ravine."

* * *

"Yeah! Feels good, doesn't it you fucking cunt?" Caleb yelled at the girl crumpled in a heap on the ground. Her hair was matted with dirt encrusted blood, and her skin was torn open and blistered across her arms and legs where the group standing over her had beaten her with a piece of scorched metal pulled from the fire nearby.

"Teach you to try and fuck somebody's boyfriend won't it, slut!" the girl standing next to her said, spitting on her to exclamate her sentence.

"I swear, I wasn't trying to sleep with him," the girl on the ground cried through split, swollen lips. "I swear."

"Whatever, you fucking whore."

Another guy stepped forward and brought his foot hard into her side.

"Yeah!" the girl standing over her yelled. "Kick her fucking ribs in."

The older man watched from atop the ridge he had crawled to when he had heard the screaming begin. He was on his weekend retreat to Joshua Tree to get away from the anxiety of the cramped city of Los Angeles. His days were spent confined to a laboratory, designing surgical accessories for a biogenetic research company. Not a luxurious job, but it paid well enough. The screams had pulled him from his small one-man tent, and for the last twenty minutes he had watched in desperate horror as the group of five younger people beat and tortured the small brunette girl in the recess of the shallow ravine.

"Fuck this," the guy they had been calling Alec said, bending over to pick up a basketball sized rock. He raised it over his head, and the man on the ridge's pupils dilated as the guy in the tight V-neck brought it slamming down on top of the girl's skull, sending a loud, wet, crack echoing through the canyon. Her body jerked, convulsing in spasms as muscles reacted to the shattered signals being sent.

The older man slid down the embankment out of sight and felt the air collapse from his lungs, and lay there under the light being cast down from the cloudless moon, his body shaking, and tears falling in streams down his face. He lay there listening to the group below continuing to laugh and battering the dead girl's corpse with a verbal assault he never imagined possible, and lay there staring at the stars above as he listened to them dig the hole to dump her body in and create a story of how they had taken Caleb's dad's yacht out for the weekend if anyone asked. He lay there with the cold earth beneath his back, the vapid realization that there would be no justice to this crime, no punishment to correlate with the viciousness of the actions he had been forced to visually endure. They would never be caught, and even if he went to the authorities, mommy and daddy's million dollar lawyers would ensure the slap on the wrist wouldn't even sting. No, he realized. This would be one time where that would not happen. If that had been his daughter, if he had a daughter, and that would have been her... No...

* * *

"I saw everything," the man said. "Everything."

"I don't know what you're talking about," Caleb said, lies slithering their way between his spit-crusted lips. "You have the wrong guy, that was my friends, not me man, please, you have to believe me."

"I watched as you and four other... people, beat and tortured that girl."

"Please..."

"A girl that was guilty of nothing; had done nothing."

Caleb looked up at him and continued to plead. "Look, I'll tell you everything, just let me go, I swear I'll tell the police what we did. I'll turn myself in, just please, let me go..."

The man turned. "I waited until you drank yourselves to sleep, and then I went to your tents and cut a small hole in the base of each one. I pumped a vapor inside them that would ensure you stayed sleeping. You see, I never go anywhere without my work, It's a habit of mine."

"Oh please... My arms hurt so bad."

"Then I went into each of your tents, and dug out your wallets. I wrote down your names and addresses, and put them back in place before going back to my camp, packing everything up, and making my way home."

"It hurts," Caleb pleaded, a small rivulet of

183

saliva working its way from the corner of his mouth.

"I waited for a month to see if anyone was going to get brought in for that girl's murder, if anyone was going to be punished. And when I realized that that wasn't going to happen, I decided it was time to do it myself." He paused, his gaze narrowing. "I have spent the last three weeks tracking your every movement. I know when you go to class, where at USC you'll be at any given moment, which room in the fraternity is yours, even your favorite fast food restaurants. I know every move you make, which is why, right now, you should be well on your way to Rosarito for spring break with your little friends. For the next week, no one will even know you have disappeared, and by the time they figure it out, well..."

It was at this moment that Caleb realized that he was not going to be able to talk his way out of this one, this time; he was going to die. He lurched back and forth, struggling against the confines that held him in the chair, the thin wires cutting deeply into his legs with every thrust, and the threading of the bolts ripping the flesh inside his forearms. He screamed, and the man turned around and made his way back to the table. He had been in the room for some time, and the cache of endorphins his body contained had been all but spent. The blinding pain coming from his extremities forced him to cease his movements and become once more, docile.

"Do you know what a biogenetic engineer is Caleb?" the man asked, his gaze working across him. "No?" He paused, exhaling a small puff of air. "We create small electronic devices that work together with the human body. My specialty happens to be devices that are used in surgical procedures."

Caleb issued a small cough.

"Now I'm sure you have noticed by now, a small discomfort coming from your lower eyelids, well... that's because while you were sedated, I stapled a little device to each one of them that is based off of something we use in a procedure called LEEP, or loop electrosurgical excision procedure." He slowly walked towards Caleb who stared at him with eyes wide and panic filled. "Now normally," he continued, "this procedure is used to cut away tissue that has become abnormal in a woman's cervix, and could possibly become cancerous later. With yours however, I have made some slight modifications."

He held up a thin, inch long, forked piece of metal with two electrodes attached to the top of it "The devices stapled to your eyelids, will send a signal to the one I am going to place in your bottom lip, and whenever moisture should pass over either one, it will send a signal to the other, and issue the equivalent of a five thousand volt shock to the corresponding side of your face that the moisture occurs, so in essence, it will be your *own* tears of remorse that will issue the punishment that will begin our very long engagement." He paused, picking up two small round objects with thin, exposed wires sticking out of them. "And these, oh these little beauties work in a very similar manner."

"Please don't, please," Caleb begged.

"Oh don't worry Caleb, these ones aren't for you. These are for your little friend Amanda, and her little sister. You see, when they wake up here, together, I will have attached these little devices to their hearts. They work in the same manner as a heart monitor, but, again, with some *slight modifications*, you see, these ones monitor the heartbeat by being connected to the right coronary artery, working in tandem sending signals back and forth to each other, so when one of their heartbeats raises above eighty beats per minute, it will fire a small targeted shock to the parasympathetic nervous system Do you follow me Caleb? It means that it will effectively send the most excruciating pain you could imagine through every nerve connected to the spinal cord, and if you didn't know, that's pretty much every nerve in your body. Not to mention the fun little fact, that it will also cause immediate urination, defecation and a few other fun side effects such as fight or flight, which will also cause the heart rate to increase, and you see where this is going." He paused, a small smile starting to form, and then disappearing quickly. "Once the heart rate reaches two-hundred, it will lock a small clamp in place, cutting off the artery, and resulting massive coronary failure. In essence, I am going to let the sisters kill each other with their own fear.

"Please," Caleb sobbed, "don't do this."

"You know Caleb," the man said, leaning in closely, and gripping a small black canvas strap next to his head. "I have heard those words come from that girl's mouth every day since I left the desert."

He pulled the strap hard, bringing Caleb's head

full force against the wooden back of the chair.

"Now," the man said, holding up the forked device in front of Caleb's face. "You'd do well to remember what I said."

He reached down and grabbed Caleb's lower lip and slowly pushed the spiked forks downwards through the top of his lip towards his chin. His body twitched from the pain and a muted scream fell out in the form of torn gasps. Then the first tear crossed the electrode.

The man stepped back as Caleb's face contorted, and he screamed as the pain coursed through the left side of his face, stopping only when the heat from his singed eyelid evaporated the tears that had worked their way out.

"Please!!!"

Another jolt.

The man stood in front of him waiting for the tears, and the electrocutions to stop. Then he made his way back to the table and picked up a small piece of yellow paper. He stood at the table reading the words to himself for a moment before turning and walking back to Caleb. He held the page up to his face and watched as Caleb's eyes scanned the paper, the pain of recognition flashing through them.

"Wha...Why is my brother's name written on there!? He wasn't there!!! Why is his name there?"

Caleb was nearly screaming, and the man stood there silently waiting for him to finish.

"You see Caleb, You and Alec hold a very special place in my heart, just as that girl's sister did to her."

He stepped back to the table and set the paper down, returning with a small spray bottle.

"You see. Her name was Michelle, and she had a sister, a little younger than her, and when they found her body through an anonymous tip, her sister..." He paused, taking a deep breath and exhaling deliberately slow. "She couldn't take it. You see, you and your friends knew nothing about this girl, you just thought you'd go ahead and exact your own form of revenge, but what you didn't know, was that two months prior, Michelle, and her sister Katie's parents were killed in a car crash; hit by a drunk driver, some rich little *fuck* like you, that because of mommy and daddy's lawyer, got off with a suspended license, and alcohol classes."

"Oh God..." Caleb sobbed, once again shooting blinding electricity through the skin covering his skull.

189

"When you and your friends," the man continued once the convulsions had once again stopped, "killed that girl, you left her sister alone, and two days later, she threw herself off a bridge." He paused. "You and your little friends, ended a family, you ended a bloodline, so that is what I am going to do to you. I am going to ensure, that everything you did to that girl, and her sister, happens tenfold to you."

He sprayed a mixture of betadine and iodine across the wounds on his arms, eliciting another scream from his captive, followed by another convulsion from his neck up.

"So you see Caleb. I'm going to be a very busy man, and you can believe me when I say this, I am dedicated to what I do, and now, this is what I do, and as you can see, it could take me years to finish this list off, but don't you worry, I will get to every name on that list."

Caleb screamed, his wails echoing throughout the wooden cabin. The man listened to them with a blank expression worn on his face, the feeling of unanswered justice building with every torn breath his captive took. Outside the wind carried the muffled cries into the hundreds of acres of trees that surrounded the man's cabin in every direction. There would be no rescue, no escape. They would all get to know the inside of cabin, even if it took years.

FALL
TO
GRACE

"Jesus is ideal and wonderful, but you Christians - you are not like him."

-Mahatma Gandhi-

Our father, who art in Heaven, Hallowed be thy name.

"I am so sorry that I have failed you."

Thy Kingdom come, thy will be done,

"I can no longer serve those that only live to serve themselves."

on earth as it is in Heaven.

"I dedicated my life to the church."

Give us this day, our daily bread,

"I have lived my life humbly, in the shadow of your grace."

and forgive us our trespasses,

"But I have lost my faith,"

as we forgive those who trespass against;

"I have lost my will to serve you on the earth you have created."

And lead us not into temptation,

"I pray to you father,"

But deliver us from evil.

"That I may serve you again in the kingdom of Heaven."

Amen.

The man standing on the roof of the seven-story hotel leaned forward and fell.

The warm night air rushed past as he closed his eyes, committing himself to whatever fate awaited him; but as he had been a member of the clergy for the last twenty years, he had a good idea what that would be.

Frances Patrick Cleary had known from the moment he was old enough to rule over his cognitive abilities that he would be a priest; that his destiny was to be paved with the soft spoken verses of salvation; his destiny, to save people, those that could not save themselves; but at this moment, five feet above the roof of a silver Honda Civic that was quickly rushing towards him, that path was no longer in sight.

* * *

"I don't care about the money John," Frances said as the bishop that stood in front of him took a deep breath in frustration. "I didn't become a priest to act as a collector for the Vatican." He paused. "For the last six months Archbishop Rivera has been breathing down my neck about increasing my intake at the parish. It is not a concern of mine. As you know John, my parish is in extremely poor neighborhood. These people are impoverished, so trust me when I say this; they are giving all they can."

Bishop Carlisle looked back at him and exhaled loudly. "Cardinal Soldano's concern is not the indigent population of South Los Angeles, it's if he can find it profitable enough to keep your; and I apologize for using this term, ghetto parish open. For the last five years, the Episcopalian's have been trying to buy that land, and I think he's extremely close to considering it; unless you can bring your numbers up. His concern isn't if they can afford to give more, it's that they aren't giving enough."

"So this isn't about the people that need our help, is it John; those that need our salvation?" Francis asked, his anger building like a river that had been dammed.

"Don't be ignorant Frances," John snapped condescendingly, "this has never been about people; you know that. This is, and has always been, about numbers." He shook his head. "You see Francis, that has always been your problem hasn't it? You are so lost in the ideals that the church is here to help the people, that you are blind to the reality; we are here to help, but our main priority is to keep the Vatican in business.

The Catholic Church is a multi-billion dollar company, a corporation that continues to run because of men like you and I, which keep that machine running. If you'd just realize, and accept that, then maybe your name would pop up when it's time to issue promotion."

"I don't want a promotion!" Francis said, bringing his fists to the table, "I just want to run my church, and help the people that look to me for guidance and assistance; those that can no longer guide themselves, those whom truly need God."

"You don't get it do you?" John barked.

"No John!" Francis said, "You don't get it. The people in my neighborhood rely upon me; their children look up to me. I deal with gang bangers, drug addicts, prostitutes; the people that society has cast away and left to rot in section eight housing and on the streets. Without me, they will be lost."

"And if you don't find a way to increase your income," John replied coldly. "So will your parish." John stood up. "I'm sorry that you can't come to terms with what is happening here Francis." He paused. "But I hope you figure it out soon, because your time here, is running shorter than you can imagine." He looked around the room, his eyes slithering across the surface. "Good bye Francis," he said, turning and walking out the door.

Francis sat there in the cool silence of his dim rectory, the harsh reality of the conversation slowly setting its hooks into the flesh of his mind. When Bishop Carlisle had left, he had taken with him something that had resided deep within him, something that once burned brightly, a beacon for those who had turned to darkness; his hope. The church he had joined those many years ago to help those who had lost their way, had itself, lost its way. How could he continue to serve an organization that only served itself? If his parish were taken from him, it would be more than just a building that would be taken; it would be his life as well.

* * *

For the next two months Francis heard nothing from the Archdiocese. There were no further visits from the Bishop, no phone calls, not even so much as a letter. He had fallen back to his routine; helping the failing community around him, giving words of guidance to youths that were destined to end up in gangs or prison, and to adults that already had. He gave his sermons and shared God's word to those who had begun to lose their way. He continued to serve, as he knew he had been chosen to do, as best he could. Then he received the letter.

Francis had just finished breaking down the folding tables the volunteers used for his Thursday soup line; his weekly donation to the homeless population that could make their way to his church from the surrounding neighborhoods. It came out of the parish budget, with a little outside donation allowing for the occasional new socks handout. He believed that healthy feet and a nourished mind were the keys to keeping a healthy soul in a roofless world.

He had moved in the last of the tables when he brought his mail in. In the stack of usual Catholic brochures and coupon books, was a letter addressed to him from the Archdiocese. He set the rest of his mail on his desk and moved to his bed, where he sat down and stared at the envelope, a nervous tension building to a crescendo in his gut, his heartbeat increasing like a silver timpani in a third movement. He played the thin white rectangle over and over in his hands before sticking his index finger in the small slot at the top where the flap folded closed, and brought it slowly to the other side, opening Pandora's envelope with a careful tear.

As his eyes crept across the page, his gaze absorbing the black words he was holding, moving back and forth like the carriage of an old typewriter with a callous precision, he felt a hollow wound beginning to open up inside of him, and a thin stream of hatred began to lace the growing laceration.

The letter was from the office of Archbishop Rivera, It read: *We are sorry to inform you Father Cleary, but the Archdiocese has come to the decision that your parish; St. Marks, has become a financial burden of which the Vatican can no longer carry. It is our decision to close your parish, effective immediately. We understand how difficult this may be for you to take in, but after numerous attempts by Bishop Carlisle to abate this situation, the decision was made to release this property. This coming Sunday will be the final mass for this congregation, after which, the doors will be locked permanently, and the contents within relocated. You are being placed on sabbatical until at which time Bishop Carlisle can find a parish for you to take over. We are sorry, and hope that you understand. God Bless.*

Francis let the letter drop to the floor at his feet. Without him, hundreds would be lost; those he had been helping would once again fall into the festering cesspool of the South Los Angeles underbelly. His parish acted as the community outreach center, his doors were open to abused children and wives, he helped dozens of people a day, and now, like a festering lesion, he was being removed.

He found himself wandering the streets that night, his thoughts lost in prayer. He felt betrayed. He knew God tested the faith of those he loved, but this was beyond. He had spent his life in servitude. He had joined the priesthood at eighteen years old, and for the last twenty years been unquestioningly dedicated to the Church.

He shuffled in a daze under the iridescent glow of the Los Angeles sky, the sounds of traffic and distant sirens the soundtrack to his walk of shame. His faith had become but a fraying strand as he realized his career was being martyred for following the beliefs he had been taught to never waiver against. Depression grew around him, enveloping him in a viscous shroud. He too now was lost.

He made his way back to the parish and called Bishop Carlisle.

"Why?" he asked when John picked up the phone.

"I warned you Francis," John replied. "I told you that if you didn't bring your numbers up, there would be repercussions."

Frances's grip tightened on the phone, his knuckles turning white beneath the thin flesh. "I have given my life to the Church," he spat angrily. "I have served God with undying devotion since I took up the cloth." He paused, his body beginning to shake. "How could you do this?"

"Oh come off it Francis," he said, irritated by the pathetic plea. "I told you what needed to be done and you ignored it. You spent your entire budget that following week, feeding homeless people, or, doing whatever it is that you do with it. You did this to yourself."

Francis's knees were shaking on the edge of the bed. "What happens now?" he asked, his teeth gritted so tight his neck was quivering.

"Now?" John responded. "Now you take a little vacation. Take some time to reconsider why it is that you're a priest in the first place, and what part it is that you actually play in the Church." He paused, exhaling with a scoff. "Maybe when you're ready to accept that this is in fact a job, and not a charitable cause with an expendable income in which to give away at your discretion, then we can talk about you returning, but until then, I think you have quite a lot to think about." He paused again before finishing his conversation. "Look Francis, it's late, and I've got a desk full of work waiting for me in the morning, not to mention that I now have to figure out what I'm supposed to do with a church full of furniture and antiques." Unseen to Francis he shook his head. "You know Francis. This is the first time in over a decade that a Catholic Church has been closed. You should be proud of yourself."

Francis sat on the bed, the phone lying still in his lap as the dial tone began to sound from the earpiece. He was broken.

He sat there, feeling as he imagined John Wycliffe and Jan Hus must have felt when they realized what the Church was becoming, only in his case, it was what it had become. They had been responsible for witch-hunts and the inquisition. They had turned countless priests into monsters, taking their basic human needs from them, and turning them into a culture of political heretics and pedophiles. Now they had destroyed him as well.

He stood up and walked over to his closet where he removed his cassock and hung it neatly, taking his cross from around his neck and putting it on the hook attached to the door. He then turned and made his way inside the church to the granite table in front of the altar, reached to the shelf below and pulled out the sacramental offerings, placing them on top of corporal and then said a Eucharistic prayer. He took sacrament, what would constitute his viaticum, and then turned to face the altar, his eyes resting upon the visage of a life sized Jesus Christ hanging from a crucifix made of wood.

He fell to his knees and prayed. He prayed for the people, he prayed for the church and members of the clergy, and he prayed for the absolution of his soul.

When he had made his peace, he stood and wiped the drying tears from his cheeks and then made his way to the front doors. He paused, turning to take one last look at the building that had been his home for the last decade, and then turned and walked to the hourly hotel next door.

He made his way up the stairwell, and opened the door to the roof.

The air was warm and still as he made his way to the edge and looked at the sprawling city in front of him.

"I am so sorry that I have failed you," he said.

* * *

Francis hit the roof of the car, sending glass exploding outwards, and the sound of crunching metal and a staccato car horn blaring into the night as the collision of his hundred and forty pound body set off the alarm.

He lay there for a moment, the pain of his impact ebbing through his body in wave after wave of excruciating pulses.

He wanted to scream but the air had yet to return to his lungs, and as his vision faded into focus he saw the orange glow of the streetlight growing and dimming with every beat of his pounding heart.

"Oh God…" He groaned, realizing that even in suicide he was a failure.

He slowly rolled to his side, his body pulling free from the folds of the crumpled metal, and fell into the gutter below.

He lay there, the horn blaring repeatedly in his ear when one of the locals from his soup line shuffled towards him. "Father?"

He stayed quiet, his mind shaking from the fact that he had just tried to end his life, his tears falling down his cheeks in a steady flow of embarrassment.

"Father are you ok?" the woman asked, stepping closer.

"Yes. I'm f… I'm fine," he whispered through labored breath.

"Father, you fell," she said, her words masking the shame of what had really just occurred.

"Yes," he said, forming the strength to bring himself to his feet. "I know, but I'm fine." He paused. "Thank you."

She nodded and shuffled away. Moments later a man came out of the hotel wearing only his boxers and a pair of sandals and yelled, "My car! What the fuck happened?!?"

"I... I don't know," Francis said, realizing that this was the first time in longer than he could remember that he had lied.

"Oh my God..." the man said, bringing his hands up to his face, and running them through his hair.

Francis turned and started back towards the sanctity of his church, the sounds of the man calling the police fading into the night air behind him.

The next morning Francis woke up and packed his only suitcase. He had no clothing other than his clerical uniforms and tab collars. He folded them neatly and placed them inside, and then made his way to the cathedral downtown, and the Archdiocese.

By that afternoon he had a small apartment in the neighborhood of Echo Park. The church had given him the equivalent of severance pay; enough for him to survive for the next year, or two if he maintained his simple life.

He had gone to a local thrift store and purchased some clothing; a few pairs of pants and some shirts, and had gone back to get settled into his small furnished apartment. A few hours later he decided to take a walk.

As he was walking down the street past the reservoir, lost in a haze of confused thoughts he saw an older homeless woman stumbling down the sidewalk. He stopped and watched her for a moment and then saw that she had changed her course, and was going to cross the street. Movement caught his eye, and he saw that there was a large van heading down the street, and that the man was yelling angrily into a phone that he was holding up to his ear. Neither of them saw each other.

Francis yelled as he began sprinting forward, the gap between him and the woman getting smaller almost as quickly as the one the van was closing. When he was feet away he jumped forward and shoved her, taking the full impact of the moving van upon himself.

There was a loud cracking sound as his body shattered the thin metal grill across the front, and the van skidded recklessly to a stop, almost flipping in the process.

He lay there in the road, his body exploding in agony as he heard the sound of the van's tires screeching once more, and the accelerated rev of the engine as it flew past him, fleeing the scene.

He slowly lifted his head to see the older woman picking herself up off the ground, and cussing him out for shoving her as she did so before shambling to the other side of the street and making her way up.

The concrete was solid as he let his head drop, thumping once more against it.

"What is happening to me?" he whispered as he heard the sound of footsteps running towards him.

"Somebody call an ambulance!" the young girl who had just approached yelled.

Francis lifted his arm off the ground and waved. "Please, don't. I'm OK," he said.

"You're not OK. I just watched you get hit by a van. Just don't move; help'll be here soon," she said, looking around. "Somebody call a fucking ambulance!" she yelled again.

"I'm fine," he said, sitting up. "See. Not a scratch."

"Wha.. How, how is that possible? I just watched you get hit by a fucking van doing eighty. You should be dead right now."

He slowly brought himself to his feet and looked around.

"You saved that woman's life," she said.

He looked up the street to see her stopped in front of a blue bin, digging a can out and dumping its remaining contents in the street before putting it into a sack she was carrying.

"God must have a plan for you," she said. "Jesus."

He stayed quiet, her words echoing in his thoughts as she made her way back to the park.

This is my punishment, he thought as he made his way back to his apartment. *My penance for attempting suicide; for going against his word, and trying to end my own life.*

When he walked back into his rented apartment he flipped the light on and made his way to his bed. He pulled his shoes off and flopped backwards onto the unforgiving mattress. He went over the incident in his head, replaying the impact with the van over and over, mixing it with the feeling of pain and unshattered bone that he had felt when he had fallen from the roof of the hotel. He tried again and again to

210

come up with a rational explanation, a way that he could have possibly survived; could have walked away from either of the incidents unscathed, but there was none. Both times should have killed him, but he was left feeling only the pain, without the release that should have followed.

Three days went by before Francis had his next denial of death.

He had returned to the parish he had left, to reclaim the rosary he had received when he had graduated from seminary. When he arrived at the church there was a thick metal chain holding the doors closed, with a rather large and unmoving lock attached to it. He sighed and decided to take a walk to help mentally prepare for the phone call he would have to make to Bishop Carlisle in order to get his property back.

He was four blocks away when he heard yelling coming from an alley that had been known to be the territory of the local street gang. As he approached he saw a younger male being held at gunpoint by two men. They were yelling for him to give them his wallet and that they were going to kill him either way. As he

211

walked past one of the men saw him and immediately aimed his pistol in his direction. He stopped in his tracks.

The gang member approached him quickly, and then slapped him hard across the face with the barrel of the gun. He felt it hit hard, and the sound of metal cracking against bone blasted inside his ears. The younger man stepped behind him and then pushed him hard into the alley towards the others.

"Looks like a two for one day," he said as they approached the other two men, one holding a knife, and the other cowering against the graffiti riddled brick wall.

"What you got for us wood?" the guy with the knife asked.

"I don't have anything," Francis said.

"Look motherfucker, we ain't playin'. We'll blow your fuckin head off. Now I'm gonna ask you again, and this time you better tell me what I wanna hear wood, or I'muna put a fuckin bullet in you."

"I told you," he repeated. "I don't have anything."

The guy with the gun approached him and put

212

the barrel to his stomach and said, "wrong answer whiteboy." And then the quiet air of the alley was jolted by the crack of a gunshot.

Francis felt like he had just been punched in the gut, and then realized that the gangster had just pulled the trigger.

He looked down and saw the white smoke still rising from the barrel, and the charred hole in his shirt where the blast had torn a hole in it, and then realized that there was no blood. It was about that same moment that the gangbanger realized Francis was still on his feet and looked down, his eyes growing wide with shock as he did.

Francis paused, and then with a speed that had been lying dormant inside of him, grabbed the gun out of the guy's hand, spun it around and put it to his head.

He wanted badly to pull the trigger, to exact the revenge he felt inside him, but he couldn't. He was still a priest, and the men in this alley were the same ones he had been fighting for years to help. "Now I want you to slowly empty your pockets and drop whatever you have in them onto the ground, now," Francis said, with a cold calm in his voice.

213

The guy started to say," Look man—" when Francis interrupted him. "Now!" he yelled. "And you too," he said to the other guy, not taking his eyes off the guy at the end of the barrel.

"Do it," the guy at gunpoint said, slowly pulling a wad of cash, and plastic bag full of marijuana out, dropping it on the ground at their feet.

The other guy did the same, and then Francis said with a layer of ice behind his words, "Now I want you to back up, turn around, and walk away. And if I see you in this alley again, I will send you to your judgment."

The guy started backing up and said, "I remember your face motherfucker; this ain't over."

"Good," Francis said as the guy was about to his friend. "I want you to."

They turned and walked away quickly and Francis leaned down grabbing the wad of cash, and crushing the bag of pot with his shoe. Then he walked over to the other man, bent down, picked up the cash and handed it to him. "You shouldn't come back here," he said.

"Thank you," the man said.

Francis nodded.

"You know they're gonna find you, and they're gonna kill you right?" the man said, shoving the money in his pocket.

"I'd like to see them try," Francis said, turning to make his way back to the street.

"Who are you?" the man asked as Francis reached the sidewalk.

He paused, his gaze glancing down the block at the now abandoned church.

"Call me Priest," he said, turning to make his way back to his car.

When he got back to his apartment he walked inside and made his way to his bed where he dropped to his knees, placed his elbows on the hard mattress and began to pray.

"Oh great and merciful God. I failed to serve you through the church, but I realize now that you have given me another opportunity, an opportunity to serve you in a different way, an unconventional way. I do not know why you have chosen me, or why I should think myself special, but if you feel myself as worthy, then your path I shall continue to walk. I swear to you, that through light and dark, pain and torment, I shall dedicate my life to helping those that cannot help themselves. I shall give my life again and again, for the privilege of saving another's. As a shepherd tends his flock, I shall watch over your children, and by your hand, will protect them with my own. I give my life to thee. Amen."

He stood up and slowly undressed, his thrift store clothing falling to a pile before him, and then picked it up and walked into the kitchen where he dumped it into the garbage can and made his way back to the small dresser. He opened the drawer and stared into it for a moment, then reached in and pulled his clerical outfit out and calmly dressed. When he was finished he made his way into the bathroom and stared into the mirror as he slid the white collar tab into place.

He took a deep breath and walked to his front door. His path was now clear. The people still needed him, the city needed him, but it would no longer be the word of God that would be their salvation, it would be him; it would be... Priest.

"Dear me! How long is art! And short is our life! I often know amid the scholar's strife. A sinking feeling in my mind and heart. How difficult the means are to be found. By which the primal sources may be breached; And long before the halfway point is reached, They bury a poor devil in the ground."

-Johann Wolfgang von Goethe, Faust: First Part-

The bar was dusky and stale, like the cheap bourbon sitting stagnant in the glass in front of the man at the bar who stared down into it like he was expecting some great miracle to come forth, or the long melted ice cubes to reform.

He'd been sitting quietly there for the last two hours by himself, after a failed attempt to get the bartender to act as his by the drink psychiatrist. He wallowed pathetically in a cesspool of his own self-pity and loathing, sitting there, on his leather swivel back throne, the king of his glass, silently scolding himself for his ever-persistent lack of talent. He had studied, read a library of books, everything from Steinbeck to King, dime novels to Dante, yet he still couldn't get past the first paragraph of his own.

Norris Buckley was a writer, or at least that's what he told everyone. He'd been left a rather sizable inheritance when his father had passed a few years prior, and had spent the last two living rent free in local cafes, leeching their Wi-Fi and reopening the same blank document on his new titanium MacBook, a *present to himself* for taking the plunge, and finally deciding to start his career as a novelist. His plan was to write the next great American novel, the only problem, his lack of natural talent stood behind every corner, wrapping his mind in an endless stream of writer's block. Today had been no different.

Norris had woken up when his alarm clock had gone off that morning; the mental one he never set, at a bright and early hour of one in the afternoon. When he slithered out of his bed, he still reeked of the night before; cigarettes and free wine supplied by a writers group he attended infrequently, once a month; second Tuesday. This one had been no different. He had sat and listened to everyone talk about their projects, and how much they had accomplished since their last get together, and when it came time for his embellishment, he responded with his usual insecurity-masking smile and said, "I don't want to get too much into it, but don't you worry, it's gonna be big." It was big all right, like the Montana sky, vast and empty. He had made his way home after that to grab his notebook and then headed to his second home, the one he didn't pay an exorbitant amount for, the one that wasn't the messy, brick walled loft apartment overlooking the dirty Los Angeles street below in the wonderful, up and coming arts district neighborhood known by its local residents as Skid Row.

As he made his way into the cafe, he said his obligated hellos to the baristas behind the counter, and slunk his way over to a back table to set up his makeshift writer's office, then made his way to the counter and ordered his equally obligatory cup of three dollar coffee, his fee for the next six hours of office rental.

He then made his way back with his cup of filtered gold, turned on his laptop and opened the document he'd been staring at for the last six months, a story about this guy, and this girl, and how they did something that led to something bigger, which resulted in something completely unexpected. He read what he had written of his newest draft, which was three lines past nothing.

He sat there for a short while, typing and deleting, looking up occasionally to see if anyone new had walked in, or if anyone was watching him work. He liked it when people saw him writing, it validated him.

For the next three hours he sat there, frustration tearing at his insides, until he felt like the nervous tension was going to make him scream. Then he stood up, a lot calmer that he wanted to, closed his laptop, put it into his backpack and drained the last of his cold coffee. He turned and left the cafe, walking back to his rented flop with his head hung low, once again defeated by the writer's curse.

When he arrived back at his loft he picked up the phone and called the only person he that could sooth his desperation.

"Hey ma," he said, falling back onto his couch with a bottle of local, brewed craft beer. "No. Yeah, I'm fine ma. No, I don't need money. Yeah. Uh huh. Yeah, I know ma." He set his phone on the table in front of him and hit the speaker button.

"So have you found yourself a nice girlfriend?" she asked.

"No ma, don't really have the time. I've been working day and night to get this book done." He said, taking a swig from his bottle.

"Oh," she said. "How's that coming along? It's the same one you've been working on for a while now right?"

"Yep," he said, "same one. It just seems like every time I sit down to write, my brain shuts down. I end up staring at a blank page for hours, then shutting my computer off and calling it quits. I don't get it ma. I studied, I went to school for this, I've read more books than I can count, but it seems no matter how hard I try I just can't write my own. At this point, I'd sell my fucking soul to be able to write."

Norris startled, a loud shattering sound yanking his attention away briefly as something heavy fell from in his bedroom, followed by a shout from his phone. "Norris! His mom said sharply, appalled to hear such vulgarities coming from her dear sweet Nori.

"Sorry ma," he said, leaning over to see what had fallen. "I just get so damn frustrated, that's all. I apologize." He paused. "Hey, look ma, I think something just fell and broke in the other room, I'm gonna let you go OK?"

"OK sweetie, call me soon," she replied caringly.

"Will do ma," he said, standing up and reaching out to hit the button to terminate the call.

"Love you," she said, as his finger was about to hit the button.

"Love you too ma."

He disconnected the call and walked towards

his bedroom, sticking his head cautiously through the square portal as if he expected to see someone standing on the other side with an axe raised in the air.

As he slowly entered, his eyes scanned the room. Then he saw what had made the sudden commotion.

Across from his bed, lying at the foot of his bookshelf was an open book, a broken bottle of wine and some scattered papers that were now saturated in the crimson hue that was slowly bleeding outwards from the jagged shards.

"Shit," he whispered to himself moving over to the mess.

He felt a cool breeze blow past, and a shimmer of movement caught his eye. He turned his head quickly to see the perpetrator of the seeping mess, and its long, flowing white accomplice.

He shook his head, feeling silly for allowing himself to get so spooked, and then walked over to the open window and pulled it downwards, locking it in place with its crude brass latch, and then pulled the thin white curtain closed, heading back to the kitchen to grab a roll of paper towels and his broom that had the dustpan attachment. When he returned he bent down, carefully avoiding the jagged edges of the broken glass to pick up the book and the papers that had been knocked down by the tipping wine bottle.

"God damn it," he said out loud, as his eyes captured what it was that had been swimming in a sea of red and transferred the image to his slightly buzzed brain and sent it back as a series of images; him sitting at his desk for days, toiling over a twelve page essay he had to write on Christopher Marlowe's Faust, a paper that had taken him almost half a semester to write, and included very carefully chopped sections of Wikipedia and Cliff's Notes, mixed with some extremely old play reviews he had found in old magazines that he was sure his literature professor would not have read.

Well so much for March, he thought sarcastically.

Three months prior Norris had purchased a subscription to a fancy wine club downtown. It was an attempt to show off his sophisticated side when engaging in conversation with the other pseudo-socialite's he liked to associate with from time to time. Now it looked like he'd have one less interesting thing to talk about; March Merlot.

He swept up the broken fragments and dumped it in his garbage can, then threw paper towels across the floor. They quickly soaked up the burgundy fluid, which he then dumped on top of the thirty-dollar waste of expendable cash.

He checked his watch; it read 6:45.

He took a deep breath and exhaled slowly, steeling himself for another writing session before making his way down to the local prohibition style mixology bar for one of his thirteen dollar nightcaps, which would be preceded by four or five Pabst Blue Ribbon's just to "get his head straight" before he went out; pregame he called it.

He grabbed two cans of beer from his vacant fridge, and then headed back into his room, slid his vintage leather writing chair in front of his desk, and sat down to write.

An hour went by and all he had to show was three crumpled cans in the wastebasket, and a fourth staring him down from next to his keyboard. He leaned back and ran his fingers through his hair, stretching his back to a satisfying series of clicks as he did. Once again he had managed to create a masterpiece of minimalist art in its rawest form, a blank, untouched canvas.

He stared at the screen for another few moments and then put both hands on the desk in front of him and pushed himself backwards in the chair, standing up as he did. He reached forward, folding his failure away and grabbed his unfinished can of salvation, downed it in two gulps, and then tossed it carelessly into the metal Ikea bin with its used brothers.

As he made his way to the main room he contemplated changing, but he liked the idea that he had a slight odor to him, his man funk as he referred to it. It added to the illusion that he actually worked for a living, after all, when you're sitting at your desk all day writing the next breakthrough novel and drinking an expensive bottle of, *What was it again? Oh, that's right, Merlot,* often, time would slip right past, and you'd forget to shower. Another masterpiece of conversational interjection he liked to use.

And with that, he grabbed his tweed windowpane blazer out of his closet and pulled a black wool knit beanie over his ears, pushing it backwards so his bangs could spring upwards in the front as he

227

stepped out. He locked his door and made his way down to the street, where he quickly walked, eyes to the ground to the inhabited part of downtown, and his overpriced glass of savoir-faire.

Two hours later Norris was sitting in his leather bound throne, his arms folded in front of him on the rounded edge of the bar, the dim red lighting washing its bordello glow over his manicured fingernails, and his watered down bourbon. He'd ordered one of his fancy cocktails, but tonight it wasn't enough to stroke his self-pity into submission; tonight he had to throw a cheap double shot of whiskey on the fire, and a second after, so he could twirl his finger in the air to feel like a real bar patron; signaling that he was ready for another.

"I'll have a martini," came a silver-tounged voice from behind the seat next to his, making him flinch slightly, "and make it extra filthy bar man, just like I like my women." The man speaking took a seat on the stool next to Norris. "I'm sorry brother," the man said , "didn't mean to startle you there."

Norris turned to look at the face attached to the Sinatra-smooth voice, and with an expression that poorly hid his embarrassment for being caught off guard, replied, "It's cool man, I just didn't see you come in."

"Yeah," the man said with a grin, "I tend to do that to people." There was a pause as the newcomer watched the bartender shake his martini. "Names... Beryl," he said, turning to stick out his hand.

"Beryl?" Norris responded with a slightly puzzled look.

"Yeah," the man responded, his perfect smile never dropping, teeth glinting in the crimson light, "tough childhood you can imagine." He paused for a moment. "And whom have I had the pleasure of startling this heavenly evening?"

"Norris."

"Norris huh?" the other smiled, thanking the bartender for his drink with a nod. "And what is it that you happen do Norris?"

"I'm a writer," Norris responded taking the last sip of his time lapsed bourbon.

"A writer huh?" the man said as he pulled the plastic stake from his drink, and delicately pulled the impaled olives off with his teeth.

"Yeah." Norris responded, downing the last of

his bourbon water.

"Bartender," the stranger with the million-dollar smile said in a friendly tone, "can I get another round for my writer friend here?"

"Oh, no. It's fine," Norris said, raising his hand from the bar to issue a weakly attempted wave to deny.

"No," the man replied, flashing his presidential smile once more, "I insist. It's the least I could do for frightening you."

"Same thing?" the bartender asked while polishing a highball glass with a bleach white towel.

"Yeah," Norris responded, glancing to him quickly, and then letting his eyes settle back to the bar, "thanks."

"Rough night?" the man asked.

"Huh?" Norris responded, caught off guard by the continued inquisition. "Yeah."

The man nodded. "Writers block huh?"

A squint flashed through Norris' eyes as he turned his head to the man who now had his full attention.

"How did you..." He paused, exhaling sharply. "Never mind."

"You know," the man began, "I knew a man once, couldn't write if the world depended on it. Great storyteller, but he just couldn't write for the life of him. Wanted to write the greatest book in the world, but in the end, had to hang it all up. It was his friends that ended up writing all his stories; taking all the credit for his work. Yeah, they mentioned him, but in the end, it was their names attached to it." He paused, taking a sip of the clouded beverage in front of him. "Never had it in me to write myself, I've always been more of a listener."

Norris nodded. "So what is it that you do for a living Beryl?"

The man smiled. "You could say I'm a... collector."

"Oh," Norris said, "like art?"

"Mmm, sort of," he replied, curling his fingers inwards and examining his fingernails, which Norris noticed were exceptionally clean, and seemed to be manicured almost to a point. "I take products my competition doesn't think are good enough, and well, find a use for them."

"Oh," Norris said, pretending that he knew

what the man was talking about.

"So how long have you been a writer Norris?" the man asked.

"About five years now," he replied, omitting the fact that four of those years was while he was is school, learning his failed craft, and that what he had been writing had been class assigned papers, and his last year of writing had been the same paragraph over and over.

"Five years huh?" the man replied. "You must be quite the accomplished author then"

"Yeah, well," Norris responded, his arrogance bleeding through, "you know, being a novelist isn't easy." He paused, taking a sip of his whiskey. "It takes a long time to find your true author's voice. But the book I'm working on right now is definitely going to be the one that launches my career.""

"Oh really," the man said, "what's it about?"

"Well, Norris began, "I don't wanna get to much into it, but it's a love story, and there's a pretty big twist at the end."

"Oohh," the man said, his smile returning, "I like a good twist ending. It's always the ones you don't see coming that are the best." He paused, "I can't wait to read it."

Norris nodded, looking down again. "Yeah, I'm just stuck on this one part."

"Doesn't it just kill you," the man said, swirling his martini, "when people with no talent can sit down and just, almost effortlessly, knock out a book without breaking a sweat?"

"Tch," Norris scoffed. "Drives me insane. No talent hacks." He took another swill of his whiskey. "What really bugs me, is I went to school for this, studied my ass off, and these assholes are landing deal after deal." He shook his head. "Unfortunately I guess it's all about who you know, not how good you are."

"Or what you're willing to give," the man replied with another velvet smile. "What would you be willing to give Mr. Buckley?"

Norris shook his head, not noticing that the man had just called him by his last name; a name that he had yet to relinquish. "Anything," he replied solemnly.

"So if I sat here, and I told you that I was the devil, and that in exchange for your simple, meaningless, insignificant soul, that I could make you the greatest writer that humanity has ever birthed, what would you say?"

Norris looked at the man he now viewed as another Hollywood weirdo, and in a sardonistic tone, playing along with the man's antics said, "I'd say, where do I sign?"

"Well," the man responded with another flash of teeth, reaching in front of him, grabbing a small paper square from the holder in front of him, and pulling an expensive looking mahogany and gold fountain pen from inside his silk sports coat; the kind that ran off of cartridge and never needed to be dipped, "I'll make you a deal. You sign your name here, and when you wake up in the morning, you'll be able to write masterpiece after masterpiece."

Norris smiled, standing up to hit the bathroom. "Why not," he said, reaching out to take the pen, "we'll call it my first official autograph." He signed his name, practicing how perfect it could be, going extra big on the loops, his hands becoming ego with the strokes. "Now, if you'll excuse me," he said in a feax-European accent, "I'm gonna go have me a piss."

The stranger nodded, a smile growing on his

face as his gaze fell to the autographed parchment in front of him.

Norris stood in front of the urinal, feeling warm release flow from him. *What a kook,* he thought.

He shook off and zipped up, walking to the sink and running his hands under the warm water. *Fuckin' weirdo's...*

He took a deep breath and made his way from the whitish yellow glow of the bathroom to the sanguine bar.

As he made his way back to the comfort of his waiting glass he noticed the man was no longer there.

He sat down and a small pile of ash on the bar in front of where the man had been sitting caught his eye. He realized that the man had set fire to his autograph.

What a dick! he thought as his brow furled and his gaze wandered through the empty bar. *Barrel...tch, stupid fuckin' name.*

He shook his head, tipping the last of his room temperature bourbon back and standing to leave.

"'Scuse me," the bartender said. "Might wanna

sit back down, the other guy bought you another round."

"Oh," Norris said surprised, "he did, did he?"

He sat back down and watched as the bar man poured another double shot of Makers over the freshly cubed ice, and set it in front of him.

He was still fucking weird, he thought as he took another sip of inspiration.

He sat there for the next half hour, sipping his whiskey, watching the bartender clean the dust off the top shelf bottles, and then eventually stood to make his way back to his flat as he called it when he wanted to sound like he had spent time in Europe.

He walked in, kicked his shoes off, and stumbled towards his writing desk where he pulled his chair out and flopped down to open his small silver opponent and hit the power button.

The screen came to life, and he opened his document, nodding off as he read over the four lines that were double spaced in front of him.

The last thing that failed writer Norris Buckley remembered before falling asleep at his vintage mahogany desk was how pathetic he felt while staring at the nearly blank page.

When he awoke he pulled his head off the desk and leaned back, his glazed, pink hued eyes coming to focus on his black computer screen in front of him through crusted eyelids.

He brought his hands up and rubbed his face slowly. "Jesus..." he whispered to himself." What the hell did I drink?"

His memory was a blur of crimson hued images, the only thing clear, a flashing smile, and a burnt pile of ash.

He swallowed dryly, his head hovering above his neck, and then reached out to hit the round button on his keyboard that would bring his mocking adversary to life.

"What..?" he whispered a breath later, as a perplexing excitement beginning to ebb inside of him.

In front of him, glowing on the light grey background was the last of a paragraph, and the words, "The End".

He stared at the screen for a moment before

reaching out and scrolling upward in the document. Before him, written in grammar that would leave even the most acute professor stunned, was a three hundred and fifty page novel, perfectly written; edited with precision.

"No way..." he whispered, as the story that had been festering in the inaccessible part of his brain, locked behind the rusted cage of writers block, unfolded before his puffy red eyes in a myriad of exquisiteness.

He sat for the next three hours reading page after page, trying desperately to pull even the slightest inkling of remembrance from his still alcohol-phased brain. It was a blur, but he knew the words were his. Then he remembered the stranger with the equally strange name, and the deal he had made.

He got up quickly, his head exploding into a shower of pulsing pain, and stars that were only visible from behind his eyes.

He checked his watch; 2:46.

His beanie was next to his front door, and he grabbed it, throwing it on quickly as he made his way out and raced to the bar he had been the night before.

When he walked in he saw a young woman behind the bar. He approached quickly and asked said, "Excuse me, I need to talk to the guy that was working last night, do you know when he'll be in next?"

The girl looked at him puzzled for a moment, and then responded in a tone that matched her perplexed expression, "I think you may have the wrong bar..." She paused. "We were actually closed last night; yearly deep clean."

"That's impossible," he answered without hesitating, "I was here, I sat right there," he said, pointing to the seat he had occupied. "I had a conversation some guy named Boris, or Barry or something. Look, I just need to ask the bartender if he remembers what we had been talking about, and if he remembers if the guy and I made some deal."

"I'm sorry," she said, searching for words, "I don't know what to tell you; there was no one here last night, and we haven't had a guy work here for a while now. It's been myself, Jaime and Denise since the new owner took over." She paused, repeating herself. "Sorry."

Norris stood there stunned. He felt like his

memories were playing a trick on him, and the rest of the world was somehow in on the joke.

"Thanks," he said, turning to make his way back outside to the blasting sun, and back to the sanctity of his darkened loft.

"That's impossible," he said convincingly to himself as he made his way down the dingy sidewalk, *I was there. There's no way I could have dreamed that, no way.*

When he got home he contemplated calling his mom and telling her what had happened, but decided that she would just end up paranoid, and that for the next six months she'd be telling him to go get checked out, and he just didn't feel like putting himself through that; he kept his words contained to thoughts.

For the next two days he avoided his computer like it contained the plague, and if he touched it, the virus would be passed onto him.

When he finally opened it back up, he saved the file to an external drive and then made his way to a local printer to have it transformed into a tangible copy, pressed and bound.

It was another week before he dared open the

240

cover to his laptop. When he did, he sat down with his usual; two aluminum companions, popped open his writing program, and started hitting keys. Twenty-three chapters later he realized he hadn't even opened his first beer yet.

He paused, astounded at the fact that the words just seemed to be forming out of thin air as his hands screamed across the keyboard in an exhausted attempt to keep up with the screaming flow of thoughts.

He popped his still somewhat chilled can open, took a heavy swig, and then dove right back in. Nine hours later he was looking at another three hundred-page novel, the excitement of his now-abated writer's block making him happier than he had been in as long as he could remember.

He called his mother the next day to tell her that the spell had been lifted, and that he had actually managed to finish his entire book in two days.

"I'm so happy for you Nori!" she said.

"I don't know ma, it's like, I just woke up the other day, and everything that had been keeping me from writing disappeared; it's incredible."

"Well I'm really happy to hear that sweetie." She paused. "Look hon, I'm running late for card night with the girls, so I have to go, but know that I love you, successful or not Nori."

"I know ma, I love you too," he replied, slightly surprised that she hadn't asked him to send her a copy of his first novel.

He made a few more phone calls; labored attempts to get friendly validation for his not so effortful efforts. He felt the hint of frustration begin to wash over him as everyone was too busy, or involved in other projects to set the time aside to read his work.

He shook it off, grabbed another two beers, and then made his way to the couch where he sat in front of the T.V., relishing in his newfound talent.

The next few weeks went by like this; writing, drinking, sitting in front of the television. In less than a month he had finished three novels and a handful of short stories. Never once did he make his way back to the bar in an attempt to find the silver smiled man.

* * *

The next ten years went by in a flash of keystrokes. Norris Buckley had become a quiet recluse, hidden away from the world around him, tucked inside his dirty loft in downtown.

He made his way out every now and then, visiting the old spots; his old watering holes for not so expensive nightcaps.

His mother had passed away a few years prior, and with his waning trust fund, he had contented him to cheap whiskey and beer, and that was only when he needed a break from the Safeway Select and PBR that stood ever so vigilant in his fridge.

Over the years his outings had become less and less frequent. He had searched for publishers, presses, agents... Nothing had panned out. He had written a library of books; a wall of literary masterpieces, but once again found himself chained by the old saying he had said in that dusky bar long ago, "It's not how good you are, but who you know."

On this night however, he sat in his weathered throne, his arms perched atop the familiar curves of a bar he had caressed countless times.

"So how's the writing coming along?" he heard, in a voice that sent a shiver of frozen lighting up his spine.

He turned to see the man he had spoken with those years ago taking a seat once again, next to his. "What did you do to me?" Norris asked in a breathed whisper.

The man looked at him puzzled for a moment, and then that languid smile grew across his face. "I gave you what you wanted. I took what was already inside of you, and simply unlocked it." He paused. "You don't sound happy?"

Norris leaned closer, his whisper shivering with anger. "I have lost everything. For he last ten years, I have sat in my box, and written book after book, story after story as the world around me fades away." He paused. "I lost every friend I had because I stopped coming out, my mother died, and I couldn't make it to her funeral because I had to finish the four thousand page epic I was working on. My life has been thrown into a blender full of story after story."

"Tell me Norris, are your works not the greatest novels that have ever been penned?" the man asked, his smile fading.

"Yes, but..."

"Then I don't see why you're sniveling. It's

pathetic."

"Wha...?" Norris asked, confused at the turn of words.

"Remember Mr. Buckley, we made a deal." Then man set the money needed to cover Norris's exquisitely small tab on the bar and stood up, turning to leave.

"Where are you going?" Norris asked the back of the man's grey silk sports coat.

The man stopped, not turning his head, but Norris heard his words as clear as if they were being whispered directly into his ear. "Like I said before Mr. Buckley, I'm a collector, so I have more collections to that I need to make. It's a never ending process, but don't worry, we'll be seeing each other soon."

Norris watched the man walk out of the bar, and stood up, making his way to the bathroom.

As he stood in front of the urinal, the smell of warm piss floating up to his face he realized something. No matter how many stories he wrote, regardless of the amount of masterful tales he wove, his curse, was that no one would ever read a word of it.

He zipped up, taking a breath full of ammonia

filled air and made his way back into the bar, walking straight for the door without as much as a glance at the inviting wood and leather he walked past, or the unfinished well liquor sitting stagnant in a glass rimmed with his drying lip marks.

He walked to his loft, his head a swirl of memories, his childhood, his years in college; the last ten.

When he got to his loft he opened the door and made his way into his writing room, or as he had come to calling it, the library of unread books.

He took a deep breath and stepped forward, taking a seat at the desk he had come to know as close as his own flesh. He opened the small drawer on his right, reached in, and pulled his hand out with a small silver, 38 snub nose attached to the end of it; protection he had bought when he moved to skid row.

"You can never be too careful Nori," his mom had said. "It's a bad neighborhood."

He held the heavy steel in his hands for a moment, shifting the weight, and then put it up to his temple and pulled the trigger.

There was a flash of light, and a *cracking* sound

that ended in what seemed was going to be an endless ringing.

As Norris's vision faded, and the part of his brain that hadn't been exonerated from his skull slowly turned off, he smelled smoke; thick and heavy, like the acrid fire of a burning sulfur mine.

* * *

"What do you make of it?" a taller man in a police uniform asked the other that was standing next to him.

"Another privileged rich kid that thinks life was too hard." He paused. "God I hate these middle class, loft renting, trust fund babies..."

"Did you run the ID?" the taller officer asked.

"There's nothing," his partner replied, "guy's got no family, no contacts newer than ten years. There's no one to call. Looks like a cleanup job for the city, and a happy landlord that gets to up the rent on another loft."

The shorter officer had moved to the shelf that spanned the wall from one side of the room to the other. "You seein' this Jerry?" he asked.

"What's that?" he answered, pulling his gaze

from the bloated corpse of another middle class drop out.

"Books, there's hundreds of em, and they all have this guy's name on em'."

"Huh," the cop said as he made his way over to his friend who was pulling one off the shelf. "Looks like we figured out what this guy did for a living."

"Not quite sure how you'd make a living off these," the other officer said. "They're all blank."

"What?" The partner said, moving forward to pull a four-inch thick book off the shelf; reading out loud as he did.

"The Dawn of a Masquerade, by Norris Buckley." He flipped through the pages of the expensive looking parchment paper, watching page after page of empty cream flash past.

The officer closed the book and put it back on the shelf, turning to the other officer as he did. "All right Rich, get the coroner on the horn, tell him to get down here, and better call municipal services, tell em they're gonna need a bigger recycling bin.

NAMELESS

"It is a fine game to play - the game of politics - and it is well worth waiting for a good hand before really plunging."

-Winston Churchill-

Day 1

11:13 a.m.

The sun was beating down upon the brim of the large hat that Geologist Richard Camp was wearing in order to block out the pounding rays of heat. The hot air washing through the thin khaki canvas had brought a thick, beaded crown of moisture below it, slowly pulling its way down his brow. He reached up and pulled the hat off, letting his hand fall to the side, and in a synchronized movement brought his other arm up and over, the light fur across his forearm wiping the wet crown away.

"So what do you make of it?" the man approaching from behind him asked; referring to the massive crater that spread out like a giant saucer in front of them.

"To be honest with you..." He paused, taking a deep breath, letting the hot desert air enter his lungs, cool slightly, and then return to the heat. "I have no idea. But I guess that's why we're here right?" The man looked down into the crater, examining the small opening that had caused the phone call that had pulled them away from their works, and drug them out to the New Mexico desert. Below them was what Richard had immediately recognized as an impact crater. It was relatively small in the world of these, probably caused by a piece of asteroid no bigger than a marble. It was roughly two football fields across, and about a hundred feet deep. It wasn't this however that had caused them to be standing under the blistering sun; it was the small, tunnel like opening that had recently opened at the bottom.

It had been two days prior that he had gotten the call from his colleague and friend John Kemper; the other sweltering soul beside him; telling him that seismic activity had popped up in the desert about fifteen miles away from Roswell, and that when he had done a satellite check of the area, he had found that one of the craters had opened up from the bottom. This was the reason he had made the phone call. Richard was a geology professor, but much of his free time was spent in caves. Geologist by day, Speleologist by night, he'd joke.

Richard looked at his friend and folded his hat,

slipping it into the small pack at his feet, and procuring a headlamp. "Least it'll be cooler when we get down there," Richard said. "Gotta love earth's air conditioning."

John adjusted the strap on his headlamp and flipped his pack across his back, cinching the straps tightly. "Well why don't we get out of this heat then," he replied, beginning his descent into the crater.

It took them fifteen minutes to make it to the bottom of the pit; plenty of time for John to voice his concerns about rattlesnakes, and heat stroke, or the truck being gone when they got back to the top.

"John," Richard said with a smile, and a small shake of his head. "I find it absolutely amusing, that you have been a geologist for the last twenty years, and you still can't go out into the field without getting all worked up over things like snakes." He stepped over a large rock, the opening into the earth just a short ways away. "How did you ever get your field work done?"

"Easy Rich," John replied with a grin. "Smith and Wesson."

"Ha!" Richard scoffed. "Well here we are," he said after a short pause, stepping towards the entrance, which was a hole that led inwards, around five feet in diameter.

He could feel cool air flowing outwards, which immediately told him that this was going to be no small cavern.

"Well let's see where this thing goes then, shall we?" John asked.

Richard nodded, hesitating for a moment as the small hairs across his arms slowly rose in the cool breeze. Then he took a deep breath, double checked his safety rope, clicked the switch on his headlamp and entered into the darkness.

11:42 a.m.

They made their way in silence for a few minutes, soaking up the quiet, cool air before Richard's whisper erupted through the small descending tunnel they were in. "It's definitely a limestone cavern. Typical for this region."

"How old?" John asked, his voice lower than Richards.

"Not sure yet, I'll be able to better judge if we find a room. Right here, there doesn't appear to be too much build up, so I'd say the part we're in right now; maybe within the last five hundred thousand years." He paused, reaching into his pocket and pulling out a glow stick, which he cracked, and stuck in a small inset in the wall. "When we get to the end I'll take some samples. I'll run em when I get back to the lab and let you know."

They continued on, and after about another thirty minutes, came to the first spot that opened up.

As they stepped into the room, Richard's headlight blasted into a large cavern. It was big enough to build a small house in, and as his light washed over the surfaces he could make out the beginning of limestone formations hanging like large teeth from the ceiling. There was a chill in the air, and he could tell that it was almost twenty degrees cooler than it was outside. He guessed they were about two hundred feet down. "Beautiful," he whispered, stepping in so that John could get a view of the room. He scouted the walls, letting the light show everything it could before making his way inwards. "Watch your step," he said. "Could be slippery."

They made their way in, carefully stepping over rocks, and around large limestone deposits that had begun their million-year climb towards the moist ceiling.

"Doesn't appear to be part of another system," Richard said, a small inset in the back wall that looked like a continuing tunnel catching his eye as he spoke.

John had spotted a small pool of crystal clear water, ringed with a rainbow of colors, and was making his way towards it, fishing a small vial out of his vest pocket as he did.

Richard made his way over to the inset and let his lamp fill the empty space. At the back of it, shoulder height was a small tube about five inches across that went straight back. He stared at it puzzled. It looked as if it had been carved into the back, as if the rock had been chipped away. He tried getting an angle for the light to enter, but it appeared to curve slightly downwards. Then a glisten caught his eye.

He heard John scuffle behind him and let out a small, whispered curse.

"You alright over there?" Richard asked.

"Yeah," John replied. "Slick rock."

"Careful," Richard said, turning his attention back to the small hole.

He fished a latex glove out of his shirt pocket, slowly slipped it onto his hand, and then reached into the crevasse.

"Sssooo long we've been waiting," a thin voice said silently in the darkness, a thought hanging in the air more than words.

As he reached the space about a foot back that angled downwards his hand came across something cold and damp. He felt around for a moment, realizing that the small tube ended at the substance, and he pulled his hand back. When he held his head back so that the light could wash over his glove, he saw that

257

there was a clear, slightly iridescent film that was covering his hand; slime the first word entering his mind.

"Sssooo long... Sssooo hungry..."

He looked at it for a moment, watching as the light seemed to make it shimmer, and for a second thought he saw it almost trying to retreat from the luminescence of the headlamp. He brought his hand up and inhaled the air around his fingers, the smell of ancient limestone and unmolested earth filling his nostrils, and then let the tip of his tongue touch the salted, calcium flavored substance.

"Ahhhhh," the voice whispered silently in the empty air, *"Warmth..."*

"Rich!" John's voice exclaimed loudly from behind him, yanking his attention away from the goo on his hand with a boom that thundered through the cavern.

"What happened!?" Richard asked, fear whipping his face around to his friend with lightning speed.

"I think you need to come see this."

Richard removed a plastic vial from his pocket,

unscrewed the top, and then pulled the glove off inside out and stuffed it into the container. He screwed the top back on and slid it back into his pocket as he made his way to where his friend was kneeling.

"What is it?" he asked as he approached. And then he saw it.

12:51 p.m.

Next to the still pool was a long decayed corpse, now nothing more than a skeleton draped in ancient tattered cloth.

"My God," Richard whispered.

"This guy's been here for a while," John said, his eyes not moving from the specimen.

"Where did it come from?" Richard asked.

"He." John replied. "It is a he, or at least he was."

"Well, how long as he been here?"

John took a deep breath. "Judging from his clothing, I'd say early pueblo, late basket maker." He paused. "I don't see any tools, or signs of dwelling, so I'd say he probably wandered in here, possibly got cutoff because of a cave in or something, and died from starvation. There's no signs of broken bones from what I can see, but I can't see what's beneath the cloth around his waist, and I don't have the tools with me to investigate properly." He looked up at Richard. "I think this just became a job for archeology."

"All right," Richard said, still staring at the

skeleton in front of his friend. "Let's get topside and call it in."

"It's tiiiime…"

They made their way out of the cave and back to the surface. They tried coming up with a slew of explanations of why the skeleton could have been there, but none of it made any sense.

"There we're a few pueblos in this region of New Mexico four-thousand years ago, but the nearest one is over a hundred miles from here," John said, putting his hat back on as they made their way up the side of the crater. "Maybe this guy just got lost, or separated, and then found the cave while the entrance was still open and headed down."

"Maybe," Richard replied. "But it doesn't make sense. Why wasn't there anything else down there with him? If he was scouting, or got lost while hunting, then why isn't there any weapons, or tools, or packs down there with him? It looks like he just wandered in out of nowhere, and made his way down there to die."

"I don't know," John replied.

"I don't like it," Richard added after a few steps.

When they reached the truck, John grabbed his

HAM radio and reached out to the university. Richard reached into his pack in the back and pulled out a canteen, taking a long pull from the cool water inside. "John," he said, tossing it to his friend.

"Thanks Rich," John said, taking a swig and then setting it on the seat as he waited for a reply to come across the other end.

"It begins..."

"Yesss... It begins..."

John reported the find, and sent the coordinates to the University's archeology department as Richard finished putting his pack away and poured some water from a jug over his head. "What'd they say?" he asked as his friend stood up and started pulling his pack and vest off.

"They said they'll get a team out here ASAP, and they'll let us know what they find out."

Richard frowned. He knew what that meant. They had just been cut off. The team would come in, lock everything down, and it'd be another three or four years before he could come back out and finish logging the cave.

"One thing for sure," John said as he slipped a

clean t-shirt over his head. "I sure the heck didn't think we'd be recovering any long forgotten corpses today."

"That makes two of us," Richard replied softly.

They made their way back to Roswell, and were on flights their separate ways by that afternoon; Richard heading back to Los Angeles, and John heading back to his department in New York.

By that evening Richard was stepping off the plane and making his way back to his lab in downtown.

7:43 p.m.

"John," Richard said, tapping the speaker button as he made his way back over to the microscope.

"Rich." John replied.

"Have you had a chance to check on our friend in the desert?"

"Not yet. I'm gonna get started on that first thing in the morning. It's almost eleven here remember."

Richard hadn't even thought about that. "Look. I need you to keep this between you and I." He paused. "That substance I found in the cave,"

"Yeah?" John injected.

"I'm looking at it through the scope right now, and it's nothing like I've ever seen before. This stuff has a structure that doesn't resemble anything on the boards." He paused, stepping backwards and removing his glasses. "I think we found something new, and whatever it is, it's reactive." He paused for a moment. "John. This stuff is alive."

"Alive?" John asked. "What do you mean alive?"

Richard was pacing slowly. "It reacts to heat and cold. It has a defense mechanism. This stuff is an organism John." He paused, putting his glasses on and then made his way back to loom over the phone, his voice lowering to above a whisper. "John, it's very important that we keep a sealed lid on this. The only two people that know about this find are you and I. We keep the findings of the cavern centered around the mysterious man, and I'll continue my research on..."

The room became silent.

"Rich? Rich are you there?"

Silence.

"Richard!"

"What if the man in the cave, and this substance is connected?" Rich said slowly.

"Connected?" John asked. "I'm not sure I follow."

"Is there any way you can get back out there?" Richard asked.

"It's been turned over to archeology Rich. Nobody except diggers are gonna be in and out of that cave for months, and forget it if they find something else and turn it into one of their protected sites." He paused. "Why do you ask?"

"I was gonna see if you could check for traces of this substance on the corpse," Rich replied, his glance turning to the microscope.

"Well," John said, beginning the formalities of his conversation exit. "I just walked in the door here, so I'll let you know what I find tomorrow. We can talk more about this then"

"Sure thing John," Richard said, his eyes still glued to the tray under the microscopes lens.

"I'm gonna have Patrick look this sample over tomorrow under the electron, and run some analysis on it." He paused. "And keep me posted on the new find."

"Will do," Richard said.

Richard stared at the dish for a few moments longer, and then walked over and pulled it off, sealing the top and walking over to place it on a shelf. There were a few other tests he wanted to run, but the technicians he needed wouldn't be back until morning. He was going to have to wait.

He put his things together and made his way out to the parking lot. His mind was whirling, trying desperately to make a connection between the man in the cave, and the living substance that had been lurking in the wall. He wasn't sure why, but he couldn't shake the feeling that whatever it was, it had been hiding.

9:10 p.m.

When Richard got home, his wife was in the living room watching TV. She had her normal glass of Cabernet, and was watching Netflix. She had just gotten hooked on the TV series Sherlock, and for the last six days, had set aside an hour and a half a night after grading her third grade class papers, to watching the exploits of Sherlock and John Watson.

"Hey hon," she said as Rich stepped through the door.

"Hey sweetheart," Richard replied, setting his bag next to the door and making his way over to kiss his wife.

"Soooo...," she started. "How was it?"

"Good," Richard replied, omitting the part about having possibly found a previously unknown living organism. "Typical limestone cavern; not too big. But we did find the body of a man that had been there for who knows how long."

"Ooohhh," his wife replied, setting the glass on the coffee table. "Tell me more."

"John thinks he's around eight to ten thousand

years old; basket weaver," he said, walking to the kitchen to open the cabinet above the fridge, and pulling a bottle of bourbon out. "We're not sure why he was there, or how he got there." He pulled the cork and poured himself a small double. "He's gonna ask around tomorrow and see what he can find." He opened the freezer and reached in, procuring three whiskey rocks which he dropped delicately into his glass, and then turned to make his way back to the living room.

"So it sounds like you had a good trip," she said, patting the couch next to her.

"Yeah," he said, sitting down, and leaning over to kiss her. "Mary Camp," he said with a smile. "And how was your day? No dead bodies I would assume."

She smiled. "No, but with a class full of third graders, the thought did cross my mind."

Richard chuckled. "You're horrible."

"I don't know what you're talking about," she said, her words falling out from behind a coy smile.

Richard immediately felt the warm rush below his stomach, and felt the heat rise in his chest. He set his glass on the table and took hers from her hand, doing the same.

269

"Hey," she exclaimed softly. "I was enjoying that."

Richard smiled and leaned closer. "And you're going to enjoy this a whole lot more Mrs. Camp."

When they had finished making love, they were lying in bed together, Mary wrapped around Richard.

"The girls and I are planning on going out for a couple drinks after work tomorrow, so I may be home a little late," Mary said, her head listening to the sound of Richards heart beating in his chest.

"That's fine," Richard replied, his words rumbling softly in her ear. "I'm not sure how long I'm gonna be at the lab. I've got something kind of important I need to work on, so it works out well." He yawned.

"Get some sleep sweetheart," Mary said, reaching up to kiss him, and then turning over click the light beside the bed. "Goodnight husband," she said.

"Goodnight wife," Richard replied with a light smile.

Day 2

7:15 a.m.

When Mary awoke the next morning, Richard was still asleep. She got out of bed quietly and started her morning routine. She had to leave by eight-forty in order to be at Micheltorena by nine for class.

She got ready and made her way downstairs to start breakfast. By the time it was finished, Richard would be making his way downstairs for work himself.

She threw together the usual bowl of organic granola, Greek yogurt, blueberries and honey, and a second for Richard, which she put in the fridge. They both usually ate at work, realizing they just didn't feel like spending the extra time in the morning to make breakfast and lunch. Besides, there was a pretty good little vegetarian restaurant not too far from the school, and the lab Richard was at had a pretty decent cafeteria, and there were plenty of places for him to grab lunch as well in downtown.

As she had just finished washing her bowl, Richard came stepping into the kitchen, sleep still

271

marked across his face.

"Hey hon," she said, kissing him as he walked past to the fridge.

"Morning," he said with an exaggerated grumble.

"We are growing..."

"Yessss. The food has returned..."

"We must feed our numbers..."

"We must..."

"Oh you hush, "she said, slapping his butt. "You slept like a log last night."

"Yeah I did," he said, flashing her that perverted smile she loved.

She blushed.

"We continue..."

"Yesssss... We continue..."

"I'll see you later babe," Mary said as she grabbed her coat and purse from the chair at the table.

"All right sweetheart," John replied, standing up from his rummage through the fridge.

She hopped into her Prius and made her way to the school. By the time she got there she could see impatient parents already waiting in the lot. She felt more like a babysitter than she did a third grade teacher. She knew it was her responsibility to teach the kids while they spent their day there, to help their minds grow, but she couldn't help feeling that a lot of the parents were just dropping their kids off so they wouldn't have to deal with them for the day. She supposed she wouldn't truly understand, because her and Richard had not had children. They had decided that they weren't comfortable bringing children into a world that was so chaotic and cruel. It wasn't right they felt; it was selfish.

She went through her daily routine, teaching basic math and English, attempting to fit in as much social development and manners as possible. Her big thing was responsibility, and being polite. More than anything else, this was what she focused on; the rest, that was purely to fit the academic schedule, but that wasn't why she felt she was there. She was there to guide the children that had been brought into this world, in hopes of possibly making just a few of them better people. "It all starts somewhere," she often said.

When the lunch bell rang, the kids blasted into the hallway, and outside to the recess area. The teachers made their way to the lounge for lunch.

"How's it going in the third?" a friend of Mary's asked as she walked in.

"Better than the fifth I would assume," Mary replied with a smile.

"Hey Mary," the woman said, returning the smile.

"Carol," Mary replied.

They moved to one of the tables and sat down.

"So are we still on for tonight?" Carol asked. "Teacher's night out."

"Of course," Mary replied. "Where did you have in mind?"

"Oohhhh," Carol replied with a large grin, her lips pulling back to expose her bright white teeth. "I was thinking Malo...?"

"Ohh," Mary replied, raising her eyebrows. "So it's gonna be a margarita night then."

"Well," Carol said. "It's been a while."

"Should I cab it there?"

"I figured we could walk it," Carol said with a shrug. "We'll leave our cars in the lot, and come back for them after. And depending on how much fun we plan on having, possibly cab it home from there."

"I like it," Mary said, pulling a cookie out of her purse, and opening the packaging.

Carol popped the top to her mocha Frappuccino drink and took a small sip. "What you got there?" she asked. "Thought you were on a diet?"

Mary smiled and glanced at the bottle in Carol's hand. "What was that Carol?" she said with a smile, taking a bite of the cookie.

She chewed for a moment, and then a small piece made its way into her throat, causing her to start coughing.

"Here," Carol said, reaching the chocolate coffee drink across the table.

Mary took it and gave a nice gulp, clearing her throat and passing it back when she finished. "Thanks Carol," she said.

"Better not die on a cookie," Carol said. "Might look bad for the rest of us dieting." She held her bottle up in a salute and took a drink from it. "So who all's coming?" she asked, setting the bottle down and capping it.

"Our numbers are growing rapidly…"

"Yessss... There are so many..."

"They have had much time to replenish..."

"So vast are their numbers..."

"This will sustain us until the others arrive...

"The othersssss..."

"They are coming..."

"Yessss... Coming..."

"Well," Mary replied. "You and I, and I think Margie and Sarah are in." She finished her cookie and made her way to the soda machine to buy a bottle of water.

"Nice," Carol said. "It's been far too long since we all went out. This is gonna be awesome."

"I think so," Mary said. "Well, I gotta go check on the heathens. See you at three-thirty?"

"Fajitas and Margaritas? You bet your little white ass," Carol said with a smile, bobbing her head in traditional southern fashion.

The rest of the day flew by and before she knew it, Mary looked up and saw that the clock read two-fifty. She told the kids to start wrapping everything up, and she shot Richard a text; Love you sweetheart, hope you have a great day.

Ten minutes later the bell rang, and she spent the next twenty minutes putting the classroom back in order. Clean at night, destroyed by afternoon, she joked with Richard.

She made her way to the lounge and waited for the other three to show.

4:48 p.m.

"Another pitcher of margarita," the waiter said, setting the plastic container down on the table next to the four glasses.

"And I said, No Jimmy, it is not physically possible for someone to break their foot off inside your bum."

The ladies laughed.

"I'd like to shake the hand of that boy's father," Carol said. "Lord knows we could use more parents like that."

"Yeah," Sarah said. "I'm so sick of the, *here you go, have whatever you want*, mentality of modern parents. Heck, when I was a girl, my parents would let me cry for hours because I wanted the new brush for my My Little Pony's hair. And you know what? As much as I hated it then, I look back on it now, and I'm a lot more patient of a person because of it."

"Yeah!" Margie added. "And we actually respect the things we have." She took a sip of her drink. "You know, the other day, one of my students was talking to another, and I heard him tell the other boy, my brother crashed his car last night, but it's OK, because dad's gonna get him a new one, and it's gonna be even nicer than the one he had." She paused. "I swear, these kids don't respect anything anymore, cause everything gets handed to them on a silver platter."

"Well here's to those few good parents left," Carol said, raising her glass. "And to one day being able to beat some sense into these kids again."

They all laughed and raised their glasses in a toast.

"Hey," Margie said. "I'm gonna step out. I'll be back in a second."

"Mhm..." Carol said, raising a suspicious eye.

"Thought you quit?" Mary said as her friend stood up.

"God!" Margie exclaimed. "You guys are like psychic vultures."

They all laughed.

Margie made her way out, and a few moments later Mary looked at the others and said, "Oh hell. I'm starting to feel that craving that comes after a few drinks. I'll be back."

She stood up and made her way outside to

where Margie was smoking. "Mind if I grab one of those from you?" she asked as she walked up.

"Last one," Margie replied, holding the thin craving outwards. "But we can share."

Mary nodded and took the cigarette, taking a long lavished puff.

"It's a really nice night out tonight." Mary said, taking another puff and handing it back to Margie.

"Yeah it is," Margie replied, taking a puff off the cigarette and exhaling into the sky. "I'm glad we got together tonight, it's been too long."

"They've rebuilt..."

"Yessss... But careful we must be."

"Yesss... Remember Roanoke..."

"Yesssss... Roanoke... They found out..."

"Yessss... They cut us off..."

"Careful we must be..."

"I still think we should do this at least once a month," Margie said.

She handed the cigarette back to Mary, who took a puff and then dropped it to the ground, pressing the delicate ember out with her shoe, and then said, "Let's get back inside, my ice is melting and I don't want a watered down margarita."

Margie smiled and held her hand out to say, lead the way.

When they got back to the table, Mary reached for her glass to find it sitting empty. "Hey?" she asked, pretending to be flustered. "What gives?"

"Well," Sarah said, feigning the voice of innocence. "The pitcher ran out, so we decided to split what was left of yours before the next one got here."

"Ladies," the waiter said, reaching out to set another pitcher down on the table.

"And here we are," Sarah added.

"We are becoming many..."

"No! We are still small..."

"We must not act yet..."

"Noooo... Not yet..."

"We must see how far we can reach..."

"Yesss... There are many more than before..."

"We wait..."

"Yess... Wait we shall..."

The group finished their evening and made their way back to the school on foot. Mary opted to walk home, and the other three called a cab.

When Mary walked through the door, she saw Richard sitting in his chair, the bottle of bourbon sitting much emptier that she had seen it before.

"What's wrong honey?" she asked.

Richard looked up, his eyes red and puffy. She could tell he'd been crying. "It's John; he's dead."

"What!?" Mary exclaimed, dropping her purse and coat carelessly on the floor and making her way over to her husband. "Oh my God. Wha.. why... how?"

He stared at her for a moment and then through a croaked voice said, "He killed himself."

Day 3

12:09 p.m.

Margie walked into the teachers' lounge and saw Mary sitting there quietly, a sandwich sitting in front of her with two bites taken out of it, her gaze on the table in front just past it.

"Mary?" Margie asked as she entered. "You ok?"

Mary looked up. "One of Richard's old friends died yesterday."

"Oh my God," Margie said, pulling a chair to sit next to her. "Is he alright?"

"As good as could be I suppose," Mary replied. "It just doesn't make sense," she added after a slight pause. She looked up at Margie. "His friend John, he'd never do anything like that. He was happy, always joking. He had an amazing job, and a wonderful family. There's no way he would have done that to them."

"What happened?" Margie asked.

"They must not find out again…"

"No… We must be more careful this time…"

"Remember Sumeria…"

"Yessss… Sumeria… No one found out…"

"Yesss… We flourished…"

"We must again… Weak we have become…"

"I don't know exactly," Mary said, her gaze falling to the unwanted sandwich in front of her for a moment. "Apparently, shortly after he and Richard had spoken on the phone, he put all of his research papers in a pile in his office, and burned himself alive with them."

"Jesus…" Margie replied.

"Yeah," Mary answered, her hollow gaze still piercing the sandwich.

"How's he holding up?" Margie asked.

"Good as he can. He had mumbled something about having to visit a water treatment plant near East L.A. when he was leaving this morning."

"Well," Margie said. "If you need anything, don't hesitate to ask you hear."

"Yeah," Mary said. "I'll be fine."

"OK sweetie," Margie said, standing up and pushing her chair in. "It's my turn on playground duty, so I'll see you a little later OK?"

"OK," Mary replied, flashing the best smile Margie knew she could muster.

Margie turned and made her way out to the playground, where she watched the kids run around and act like hooligans for the next twenty minutes. Then she herded them back inside and finished out her day.

6:15 p.m.

"Hello my sexy, ebony queen," Margie's husband Carl said as he walked into the kitchen from work.

"My ever so faithful and indentured servant," she replied with a smile, pulling him in for a passionate kiss, their tongues caressing each other's with a soft exchange of vibrant energy.

"So many…"

"Yessss… Our food surrounds us…"

"Surrounds us it does…"

"Our numbers grow with every moment…"

"Yess… We have been patient…"

"Patient we have been…"

"Not much longer…"

"So many…"

"Yessss… Many…"

"And how was your day my love?" she asked, turning the flame to the pasta that had been boiling on the stove off.

"Good," Carl replied. "I think your sexy husband might just be in line for a promotion."

286

"Oh really..." she replied with a smile.

"Oh yeah," he said, moving behind her and letting his hands move slowly around her waist to her stomach, his breath grazing the back of her ear. "And you know what that means," he whispered.

"Mmmm," she replied, pushing her pelvis back.

His hand started to move down and she pushed back with her waist. "Uhn-uh mister. You haven't gotten that promotion yet."

"But I'm going to," he replied with a smile, making his way to the fridge to grab a Dos Equis out.

"Well then, we'll talk about that, then."

"Fine," he said, grabbing a seat at the table.

"You remember Mary's husband Richard?" Margie asked.

"Yeah," Carl replied. "Nice guy; kinda quiet. He's like some scientist or something right?"

"Geologist, but yes, him." She turned around and brought the pasta she had been mixing up, and started scooping it onto the two plates at the table. "A really good friend of his killed himself the other day; burned himself alive in his office apparently."

"Jesus," Carl replied. "What the heck is wrong

287

with people these days?"

"I don't know," Margie replied. "But she took it kinda hard." She paused. "I felt really bad for her you know. Never a good thing to find out. I think she knew him pretty well too."

"Damn," Carl replied, taking a sip from his beer.

They ate the rest of their meal and then made their way to the couch to relax with a movie on Netflix. The rest of their evening was spent peacefully in each other's arms before they made their way upstairs, made love, and then went to sleep. When Carl awoke the next morning, he was out of bed in a flash.

Day 4

8:15 a.m.

"Oh fuck!" Carl exclaimed, realizing that their alarm hadn't gone off. "Babe," he said, shaking Margie awake. "Power went out. The alarm reset. It's eight-fifteen."

"Oh shit," she replied, sitting up quickly.

Carl got dressed with lightning speed, and then grabbed his cellphone. "I really hope this doesn't ruin my promotion." He hit the button and waited for the answer. "Yeah, Carl Adams here, look, the power went off at my place, tell Mr. Summers that I'm on my way. I'll be there as quick as I can." He paused listening to the voice from the other end. "Really? Oh my God. That's the best news I could have heard today. I love you Grace. Thanks. See you in a bit." Carl dropped the phone on the bed and took a deep breath, exhaling loudly.

"What's up honey?" Margie asked.

Carl smiled. "Mr. Summers got called off this morning. Something about an emergency at one of the plants we insure."

"Oh my God," Margie said while pulling her slacks on. "That's great."

"Yeah," Carl replied. "Of all the days for him to not be there, this is it. I am one lucky man."

"All right babe," Margie said, rushing to grab her purse. "Gotta run."

"Have a good day babe," he replied, giving her a quick kiss.

"You too," she said as she ran out the door.

Carl got ready for work at his regular pace, allowing his heart rate to slowly lower to back to normal. Then he made his way out to his car, got in and headed towards his office in Westwood. He worked for an insurance company that dealt mostly with industrial plants and commercial manufacturing.

As he was heading towards the freeway from Echo Park, he decided to stop at the coffee shop on the corner of Sunset and Alvarado; now that he had some extra time.

He walked into the shop, and while standing in line, recognized the man standing in front of him.

"Jim?" Carl asked.

The man turned around and with a look of surprise, replied, "Carl. How you doing man?"

"Good," Carl replied. "Had some extra time this morning so I decided to grab some coffee on the way in."

"They have covered the entire planet…"

"Yessss… Spread they have…"

"Much reserves this time we shall store…"

"Yess… Energy to last…"

"How's the missus?" Carl asked. "Margie mentioned they went out the other night."

"Oh yeah," the man replied. "Sarah's doing great."

"Awesome," Carl said, nodding to the counter to let his acquaintance know that it was his turn to order.

"Like the Olmec's this shall be…"

"Yess… The Olmec…

"And the Moche…"

"Yess… A feast…"

"Yessss… Feast it shall be…"

"They will come…

"Yess… Come they shall… And wait we shall…"

291

"Yessss... Wait we shall..."

"Jim took his coffee and shook Carl's hand. "Well, it was good talking to you, but unfortunately, I'm on the same train as well; heading to work."

"All right Jim," Carl said, watching his friend leave.

9:53 a.m.

When Jim arrived at work, he got out of his truck and saw his crew waiting for him in front of the building.

He walked up greeted them, and then started discussing the plumbing job they had to do that day.

He went over the details and then told the guys he'd meet them on the site.

"Mind if I ride with you Jim?" one of his employees; Paulo, asked.

"Sure man," Jim replied with a smile, "jump in."

They got in the truck and started making their way to the site.

"You hear about that shit that happened yesterday?" Paulo asked Jim from across the cab.

"Ensure our survival when we have fed we must…"

"Yess… We must…"

"No man, what's up?" Jim replied, taking a sip from his cup.

"The first… The one that brought us back…"

293

"No longer it is… Sacrificed it has been…"

"Some scientist guy went to a water treatment plant near East Los and threw himself in one of the outlet ducts."

"Our colony..?"

"Safe it is… Where it left it it is…"

"Then hide again we must…"

"Yesss… Hide we must… Until they arrive we must…"

"What?" Jim replied, flashing him a puzzled glance.

"Yeah," Paulo answered. "Apparently the dude had been there, stuck against some grate for hours before they found him."

"A millennia it has been…"

"Yesss… But a new home this shall be…"

"Harvest we can… These creatures we must…"

"Damn," Jim said.

"Yeah," Paulo replied. "And you wanna know the fucked up part. A third of Los Angeles is gonna be drinkin' water some dead guy was in."

"We must rebuild…"

"Rebuild yesss… We must…"

"You gotta be shitting me?" Jim said appalled.

"Yeah dude," Paulo said, taking a drink from a water bottle and holding it up. "I wouldn't be drinking from the tap for a while if I were you."

5:46 p.m.

When Paulo walked through the door to his house, the sound of screaming reached his ears.

"What the fuck is going on in here?" he yelled, making his way into the living room where his two youngest sons were fighting over an Xbox controller.

"We have enough..."

"He took his turn and wouldn't let me have mine," his youngest said, immediately followed by the older defending himself. "Nah fool, I hit reset, so that turn didn't count."

"We need more..."

Paulo walked in and pushed the power button on the console.

Both his children exclaimed loudly.

"No. Enough there are... Greedy we cannot be... There must be creatures left to build again... Starve we will if they cannot... Survive we must... Until the others arrive..."

"Next time I see you arguing over this thing," Paulo said, watching his wife walk into the room. "It's going to Goodwill."

"But daaaad!!" the older exclaimed.

"No buts. I'm being serious. I'm sick of this." He paused. "You think I wanna come home to this? Huh? I've been ankle deep in mierda all day so I can buy you shit like this. You need to listen to your mother, and stop actin' like a couple little bitches."

"When..?"

"Feed when the bright star rises we shall... Fill ourselves we shall..."

"And then back to the darkness we shall go..?"

"To the darkness we must... Safety only in darkness there is... Too fragile we are..."

Paulo sent his children to their rooms and pulled his wife in close. "I'm tellin you babe, just one good chancla to the ass, that'll put them right in place."

"Oh stop," his wife said. "Always actin like the badass."

"It's cause I am eh'," he said, nodding his head upwards.

"Hungry we are..."

"Yesssss... Hungry... Their energy we shall consume..."

They smiled at each other and then kissed.

Paulo pulled his wife into a hug, and held her until the sound of a door slamming above made him pull back and shake his head. "I swear babe, one day I'm gonna kill those little bastards..."

"Yesss... Consume we shall... Till none are left..."

"NO! Survivors there must be... A carrier to darkness there must be... Our legs they are..."

His wife smiled. "Go take care of it, I'll pull your dinner out of the oven."

"That's what I'm talking about," he said as he made his way to the stairs, yelling, "Which one of your little asses am I about to have to beat."

"Yesss... Legs... Survivors... Until the others arrive... Then no more they shall be..."

His wife smiled and made her way to the oven, opening the door, and pulling out the plate of food inside.

"Yesssss... A feast it shall be..."

Day 6

2:23 p.m.

The scorched husk of a man made his way slowly through the sands of the Mojave Desert. He had been walking for the last three days. His skin was blistered, and the redness of his eyes glared at the sand through the sunken lids.

His movements were methodical, taking step after step, his breath coming short and ragged through torn, split lips.

He was carrying a small glass petri dish with a screw on lid, was wearing a tattered white lab coat that had a nametag printed across the front in blue lettering that read; Patrick and was hissing the word Croatoa over and over with each labored breath.

"Rest we must now... Wait we will... They will rebuild, and we shall rise again to feed..."

THE
SEED

"Reality is never as bad as a nightmare, as the mental tortures we inflict on ourselves."

-Sammy Davis Jr.-

The rain was falling in sheets, blowing past the floor to ceiling window in a darkened shower. The man lying in bed could see it silhouetted against the stormy night sky through the haze of silver light trying desperately to fill the room.

He was drunk again.

He was always drunk.

As he lay there, staring though the dripping glass past his balcony to the moon bathed cove below, his wife came walking quietly out of the bathroom. His eyes pulled away as he saw her outline approaching him. As she started to crawl onto her side of the bed he could feel the soft tingle of arousal stirring in him.

It was the booze.

He pulled her towards him and began to kiss her deeply, passionately. As he firmly pulled her under him and began to slide her pajamas down she paused and asked him, "Do you love me?"

"Of course," he replied through a bourbon haze. He could still taste the molasses burn in his throat.

"Is this what you really want?" she asked with a stir of reluctance in her soft voice.

His response was the saliva-based lubricant

being slid over his whiskey-hard cock. He rolled over and pulled her on top of him, allowing her to take control and ride him softly for the two minutes it would take him to drunkenly finish. As she pulled herself up and down to please him he struggled to maintain his erection. His mind had wandered somewhere else; to someone else.

The thunder didn't cease

As he erupted he pulled her in close and then moved her softly to the side and made a weakened attempt to stand. The world was spinning around him. On the second attempt he was able to bring himself to his feet, and with drums pounding against the walls of his skull began to stagger towards the bathroom. He made it a few steps before realizing that the covers had wrapped themselves around him and were beginning to trail off the bed. In a frantic jolt his wife darted off the bed and towards him.

"I need those!" she said, fear thickly glazing her words.

"...Wha..?" he responded through the haze.

"They'll return," she whispered, her gaze flashing like a dagger down the hallway.

303

"Who... What?" he stammered, puzzled as he began to allow the enveloping cloth to be pulled gently away.

"The ones that were here before," she whispered, her eyes still locked to the hall.

He had no idea what she was talking about. The only words that could form through the still in his mind began with crazy...

He watched as she backed up and pulled the blankets back onto the bed with her, pulling them over her head. Then he turned to stumble into the bathroom.

It was a mess. The entire garbage can had been strewn across the floor from one end to the other, and as he grabbed a towel and begun wiping himself off, he noticed what was lying in the base of the tub.

"Oh shit..," he whispered to himself under his clouded breath.

In a loosely thrown pile were the spoils of his last week. A handful of used condoms from him and his mistress.

Was she on her rag, he thought as the sight begins to register.

How the hell is this possible? he wondered frantically. *How could I have not taken the trash out...?* He leaned over and grabbed the tipped can and began to make a drunken attempt at cleaning up before the spinning forced him to stop and he was left with no choice but to stand or fall face first into the tile.

He could hear thunder rumble again.

He set the can down and began to make his way back into the room. The rain had begun falling harder.

As he made his way cautiously towards the bed, guilt began to flood through him. *How could I have been so careless...?*

He saw his wife sitting silently on the bed, legs tucked up in front of her, her head hung low to her knees. He could feel pain emanating from behind the loosely draped sheets. As he approached the flash of a shadow caught his eye from down the hallway and an icy shiver slowly worked its way up his vertebrae, spreading outward like frozen wings across the top of his back. He tried desperately to give a forced, "I'm so sorry", but his words were whispered in silence. He turned to make his way down the hall.

As he shuffled past his wife, lightning filled the

305

room with a brilliant flash, and he could see that his wife had pulled the covers over her head again, leaving her form posed on the bed like an unfinished sculpture, draped in the thin cloth.

He lowered his gaze and began down the hallway.

Thunder exploded from outside again.

As he got to the guest bathroom he turned and looked down. Seeping outward from the sink was a growing puddle of water. *The rain must be getting in...*

He slowly walked forward, lightning spreading its gaze once more through the small window above.

He made his way towards the spreading liquid and bent down. He could feel the presence before he heard it.

SLAM!

There was a heavy thud as something heavy hit the door behind him, and he spun to see a shadow standing in the doorway. The shadow was his.

There was a tortured scream down the hall as the woman in the other room slowly rolled to her side, pulling the cold sheets delicately closer to her. A thin smile had begun to work its way towards the edges of her lips as a tear worked its way down the bridge of her nose towards the bed. She could feel the warm seed of a dying man working its way in a thin viscous strand down the inside of her thigh as the house once again became silent.

Outside lightning flashed.

"A sword-wielding exorcist teams up with a pyrokinetic werewolf to take down the four horsemen of the apocalypse in order to save her pet T-Rex."

-Jack Sy-

Jack Phoenix had been in school when the police pulled him out of class and told him that his father had been killed. He was ushered out of chemistry and greeted solemnly by two uniformed officers in the hallway.

"We're sorry to have to tell you this son, but your father has been shot. He's dead."

The officers had told him that they were sorry, and that they were going to do everything they could to find the person that had done it; the usual speech. It was all a blur.

They were lying; they never cared.

He had sat quietly in the principal's office for the rest of the day, his head hung down between his slouched shoulders, his gaze burning a hole through the speckled carpet at his feet. He was empty.

His mind raced over the memories of his father, always smiling and happy; coming home every night smelling like oil and grease, a mechanic's cologne he'd called it. He thought about their annual camping trips; their yearly *get the hell out of town* trips. He thought about his dad sitting at the kitchen table, silently mourning over the loss of his wife; Jack's mother, six years ago, and how he had stepped up to ensure that Jack could still have a good life, and everything he needed; from new skateboard decks to the latest issues of Justice League and Spawn.

His world had been shattered that morning, what little joy he had in life torn from him at the end of some faceless barrel.

Solitude washed over him, and as he made his way home that day he left all remaining hope and joy on his principal's carpet, in the form of a small salted puddle of lament.

* * *

Jack sat in his house that night, waiting for his aunt to pick him up. She wasn't off work until nine, and that gave him time to wander his house in a daze, lightly grabbing the things he needed for the next two days until he could come back and grab more of his belongings.

His aunt had agreed to take him in; it was only six more months until he turned eighteen, and could move back into his house, which his father had left to him. Six long months before he would have to return, and immerse himself in the painful memories.

He gathered clothing, and his bathroom supplies; his toothbrush, razor, and hair gel. He put it into his backpack and then made his way to the back, to his father's room.

He stood in the doorway staring at the empty room, awash in memories, and then slowly made his way to his bed. He collapsed, his face buried in his pillow; enveloped in his smell, and cried. He sobbed until his eyes were all but dehydrated, stinging rivulets of salt beneath his lids, and his stomach was shaking from the tenseness. He lay there inhaling the memory of being hugged, and woken up with coffee and donuts before school. He stared across the room at the picture on his dresser; the one taken on their last camping trip, of the two of them standing in front of the crystal blue waters of Lake Tahoe, fishing poles in their hands, and bright, luminescent smiles on their faces.

He slowly sat up and let his eyes graze around the room before standing up and walking towards the dresser. He reached out and took the picture, holding it tightly against his chest, and whispered, "I miss you so much dad..."

Then he turned and walked slowly back into the

hallway, another reserve of tears working their way down his cheeks, and set the picture on top of his bag.

For the next two hours he sat in the darkness until he heard his aunt's car pull into the driveway, and then brought himself to his feet, and made his way outside.

As they sat silently in the car, heading to his aunt's house in Echo Park, his breaths came in short, shallow gulps. He couldn't bring himself to say anything out of fear of bursting out in sobs again. His aunt had given him the space he needed, and wasn't pushing for a verbal exchange; she was just driving along, her eyes staring out the window, her arm reaching across the console, with her hand on his leg.

* * *

The next day was a blur. He didn't go to school, he just sat in the spare room of his aunt's house, occasionally getting up for water, or to stare out the window at the cars passing down Sunset Blvd. He didn't want to go out, and he didn't want to stay in, so he resolved himself to eventually making his way to the front porch, and adjusting to an afternoon of a combination of the two.

The day went by; he only cried silently.

* * *

On the third day, Jack decided to make his way to the Rampart Division to speak with the detectives that had been assigned to his father's case. He knew this much because his aunt had been asking a lot of questions. She had been the one talking to the police in the beginning, and the one they had told about certain procedural protocols, and ways that things like this went.

Jack had almost snapped when his aunt had told them they referred to his father's murder as, things like this. *Things!* His father was not a thing; he was not some stolen car, or graffiti'd building.

He walked into the station and told them who he was, and asked if he could speak to the detectives to find out if they had found any information. A few minutes later a middle-aged Hispanic man with a cheap, suit outlet style two piece came shuffling out from the back.

"Why don't you come into my office," he had said, turning before a response could be received.

Jack followed quietly behind him. "Is there any

new information about my dad?" he asked.

The detective stayed quiet, and when he reached the end of the hall, stopped and opened a door, ushering Jack into the small, stale smelling room.

They both sat, and the detective looked at him from across the desk. "Would you like some water?" he asked.

"No," Jack replied, "I'd like to know where we stand."

The detective nodded. "Look," he began, folding his hands in front of him on the cheap, Ikea style desk. "There wasn't much evidence left at the scene. We can tell that it wasn't a robbery, because nothing was taken. Your father still had his watch; his wallet was still in place, with cash and cards inside, even his pocket change was untouched, so what we're trying to do, is establish a motive, but to be honest with you Mr. Phoenix, it's really looking like a case of wrong place at the wrong time."

Jack stared across the desk at the unempathetic suit staring blankly across at him. "So that's it? You looked; you didn't find anything, and now nothing. My father was murdered, and you're just gonna tell me, sorry, it was just the wrong place at the wrong time?" Jack was furious. "What the fuck do guys get paid to do here?"

"Look kid," the detective said, stiffening up. "We've asked all the people in the surrounding houses if they heard of saw anything, we've tried running a trace on the bullet that killed him, and we've tried retrieving video from traffic and local surveillance cameras, but unfortunately, the neighborhood you live in is run by a pretty vicious street gang, Coronado Street. I'm sure you've heard of them. It's also the same the street you just so happen to live on, so getting anyone to say anything, is like asking them to order their own death sentence." He paused for a moment, taking a deep breath. "We're doing what we can, but you have to understand, the people in your neighborhood are afraid of them. And rightfully so. Coronado Street has run that neighborhood for the last thirty years, and has a lot of powerful connections. Their member's families run the local markets, and work at the local restaurants. They have eyes and ears on everything. No one is going to give up any information that would put their own families at jeopardy, I'm sorry, but it's the hard truth."

Again that blank stare.

Jack hated this man.

Jack took a deep breath and stood up.

"I'm sorry," the detective said to his back.

The door closed behind him, and he made his way quickly out of the station, hooking left on Eighth Street and heading towards downtown.

He made his way to Pershing Square, the spot he enjoyed going to think, and found a cement bench that wasn't occupied. He sat there for the next two hours, watching traffic, and a homeless woman feed pigeons.

Time crept by, and eventually he brought himself to his feet, and made his way to the coffee bar down the street; G&B. He walked up, and the man with the glasses and the smile behind the counter looked up. "Hey Jack, the usual?" he asked with his unpracticed politeness.

"Hey Charles. Yeah."

The guy behind the counter turned and made his way to the back, returning with his cup of iced Ethiopia. "Here you go Jack." He paused. "You alright man?" he asked.

Jack paused, forcing the tears to stay behind his lids. "My dad died three days ago."

"Oh," Charles said, "I'm so sorry."

Jack nodded, reaching for his wallet.

"No, no." Charles said, waving his hand. "Don't worry about it." He paused. "Look man, if you need anything, please, don't hesitate to ask. You know where I'm at. If you need someone to talk to... I'm here for you."

"Thanks Charles," Jack said, nodding. "Just gonna take some time."

"All right," Charles responded, flashing a light smile behind the look of concern. "You take care of yourself yeah."

Jack made his way down the street, and took a walk through the Second Street Tunnel. The air was cool, a nice momentary release from the dry July heat.

As he walked down the street his mind fell back to the conversation he had with the detective, and how the gang had everyone in his neighborhood so afraid, they wouldn't even help a neighbor find out who killed his father. If he had seen something like that happen, he would have gone to the police in a heartbeat. Did these gangs have so much control over the people that they could do anything they wanted, and get away with it; no repercussions?

He walked on, lost in thought, and it wasn't until he was well on his way down Beverly that he realized he was on autopilot, and was heading to his house. He paused, and then decided he might as well head there and grab his clothes. He only had enough for a couple days, and would eventually have to go there anyways.

As he walked down Beverly, things started to become more prominent to him. He started seeing tagging that he had until now, just walked or skated past with no notice. He began to notice how much there was, and putting the names attached into memory. He and his friends had used to laugh, and call it chicken scratch, but now as he gazed across it in passing, the scratches held a more ominous presence, turning to gouges across the walls, markings that stood as warnings; beware all ye who enter here.

Jack opened the front door of his house, and almost instinctively called out, "I'm home", and then

319

stopped, letting his words fall to a whisper, his gaze lowering to the floor for a moment.

He closed the door and made his way to his room, where he pulled his camping bag from his closet and made his way to his dresser.

When he had finished loading his clothes, he took a seat on his bed and soaked in as much of the room as he could. It would be another six months until he would be back, and when he did return, it would be much different.

As he sat there, his eyes wandered up the wall to the Justice League poster hanging above his dresser. He stared at it for a moment, and then the bone-white skull on the wall to his right caught his eye. It was a poster he had gotten at Comicon with his dad the year prior, which was from the Punisher series. It had the Punishers t-shirt draped over the side of a brick wall, pockmarked with bullets, and a pile of empty shell casings below it. He stared at the poster for quite some time. He wondered why no one did things like that. Why did nobody take a stand against the gangs, or organized crime on their own? Why did they just let the police, that were just as corrupt as the gangs in their own, sit by and watch as these criminals, and gangsters hold the city's neighborhoods in a headlock. The people in this city were losing, and the gangs were on top, with full control.

As he stared at the poster he tucked his fear away, letting anger and hatred come full force forward, and made up his mind what he would do. If the police wouldn't find anything out, he would ask questions of his own. He would find out what happened, and he would tell detective apathy himself.

He finished gathering his things, and then made his way back to his aunt's house. He now saw the writings on buildings and dilapidated structures and back walls for what they truly were. They were markings designed to instill fear; but he was no longer afraid, he was angry; vengeful.

* * *

The next morning he awoke and made his way downstairs. His aunt was cooking breakfast, and the smell of bacon frying had hit his nose before he had even entered the hallway.

He walked in the kitchen and said, "Morning."

His aunt turned with a smile and replied, "Good

321

morning Jack." She turned and continued to flip the bacon, pausing to lift the cover of the pan her eggs were cooking in. "Are you ready to get back to school?" she asked.

She had kept quiet this long, but he could tell she was anxious to see him reintegrate himself and try and move forward.

"Next week Doris," he said, walking to the coffee pot and filling his mug. "Gonna take the next couple days before I go back. Not sure if I'm ready yet to answer the questions I know I'm gonna be asked."

"Oh. OK," she replied, turning to flash him a smile. "Whenever you're ready honey; there's no rush."

'Good' he thought to himself, 'cause I'm in no hurry.'

He sat at the table and drank his coffee in silence while his aunt finished cooking their meal. As she set his plate down, he asked her, "Doris?"

"Yeah?" she replied, pausing.

"How long did it take you to get over Uncle Darryl's death?"

She took a deep breath and then turned to make her way back to the stove. "I don't think you ever get over the death of someone you love, I just think you eventually learn different ways to live with it."

She turned and made her way back to the table. "Not a day goes by that I don't miss your uncle, or that I don't think about him." She paused, looking down into her coffee cup. "It just gets a little less painful as time goes on."

Jack stayed quiet, and finished his breakfast. He felt bad for asking, but the question had been shredding his insides attempting to escape, and he couldn't hold it back any longer. The answer wasn't comforting.

He finished his breakfast and made his way to the sink, setting his plate and mug inside and kicking the water on to clean them.

"Oh, you can just leave them there Jack," his aunt said from the table. "I'll take care of them."

"OK," Jack replied, turning the water off. "Thanks Aunt Doris."

It was a little past ten o'clock when he made his way out, his mission clear in his head. He was going to head to his neighborhood, find the local gangsters, and get his own information from them. He wasn't afraid, and knew that they bled just the same as he did. They were not going keep him from finding out the truth; they no longer intimidated him. His mind flashed to the poster on the wall, and his courage built up as he walked towards his house.

A half an hour later he reached the corner of Temple and Coronado. He turned down his street, and slowly walked towards Beverly. He was stalking his prey, looking with pursed lips and squinted eyes down every driveway and alley he passed. It was a few blocks later when he found his mark; four gangsters siting in an alley, the smell of marijuana and grape blunt wrap wafting outwards.

He entered the alley and made his way towards them. As he approached one of them stood up from the small wall he was sitting on and turned to him. "Wusup homie, you lost or somethin'?"

Jack stopped. "Four days ago my father was shot on his way home. I wanna know who did it, and why some pussy motherfucker would shoot an old man?"

"What the fuck you just say motherfucker?" the one who just stood said, walking towards him.

Now fear struck.

"You think we shot your old man fool?" he said, stopping less than a foot in front of Jack's face, his friends walking up behind him. 'You're gonna walk into our fuckin' alley and accuse us of killing your fuckin' dad?" He paused, throwing a glance to the guys behind him who slowly started to circle.

Jacks fist balled up.

"You made a big fucking mistake fool," the gangster said, swinging his arm in a typical haymaker fashion.

Jack ducked quickly and brought his fist up from below, connecting it squarely with the baldhead's jaw.

The sweet spot.

The gangster staggered and fell, and Jack spun instantly bringing his elbow up to the attack he knew was coming from behind. He had spent the last six years studying Kenpo, and mentally prepared for this every day.

He felt the soft tissue covering skull impact the bone of his elbow, and saw as another one staggered backwards, his feet slowly coming out from under him and gravity won its battle with his quivering knees.

Then he heard the telltale clack of a handgun

slide locking into place.

Jack froze. He slowly turned to see one of them standing there with a black pistol aimed at his face. His hands slowly came up.

The guy he had hit first was getting to his feet, and was rubbing his jaw, shaking the stars from his vision.

"Oh you fucked up homie," he said as he stepped forward and swung hard, bringing his fist against the side of Jacks face.

He fell.

Jack hit the ground, flashes of light streaming across his vision as the other two still standing stepped forward and joined in on the ground and pound that was being delivered. They punched and kicked him until his eyes were nearly swollen shut, and his ears were hearing nothing but a muted ring. Every breath he took felt like knives were pressing into his sides; broken ribs he guessed.

As he lay there taking gasped breaths, tasting the blood working its way backwards into his throat, the one with the pistol stepped forward and looked down at him.

"You know what fool, I killed your old man." He paused, glancing at his partners. "That fuckin' maricón thought he had some balls; tried to come up in here and tell us he was gonna start callin' the pigs if we came down his block again. Fuck that! That fuckin' puto won't call the cops now, will he?" He raised the pistol and aimed it at Jacks chest. "And you won't be either. Coronado Street ese'!"

The last thing Jack felt before the blackness faded in around him was his chest lurch, like someone had stood over him and dropped a bowling ball directly onto him.

He heard the pop, and felt his breath get taken away, and the sounds of the alley fading into the distance.

* * *

When Jack opened his eyes, a world of white slowly filled his gaze. Through the blur he could make out what appeared to be a ceiling, with a luminescent light panel in it above his head. He heard the rhythmic beeping of a heart monitor next to his head, and after a moment realized he was in the hospital.

He lay in bed for quite some time before a

nurse walked into his room, and he managed a small, whimpered, "uhh."

His chest felt like it was on fire, and as the nurse walked over to him he attempted to talk again, but she said, "Shhh. Don't speak."

She reached down and checked his wrist, and then looked at the monitor. "You know," she began. "You're lucky to be alive."

His brow furrowed, his only way of silently asking why.

"When they brought you in, you had been beaten pretty badly." She paused again, her eyes glancing at his chest, and then moving back to his. "You were shot."

He took a shuddered breath.

"It barely missed your heart. Another eighth of an inch and you wouldn't be here right now." She smiled. "It looks like you have someone watching over you."

She grabbed the clipboard next to the bed and scribbled something down, and then turned back to him. "You lay here and rest, and someone will be in here in a bit to check on you OK?" She turned and made her way out, leaving him to the sound of the heart monitor, and the sterile smell of the stagnant room.

Jack lay there trying to piece together what had happened. He remembered walking into the alley, and he remembered the faces of the guys he had approached and their voices, but after that, it was blank.

He was in the hospital for another four days before he was released. The detective that he had spoken with about his dad had come in and asked him some questions, but he told him that he didn't remember what had happened. His aunt had come in in tears, talking about how it was time to move out of the city, and how they needed to go somewhere away from all the gangs and violence, but he knew she was wrong. There was no getting away from it. This wouldn't stop until someone made it stop.

He sat in his aunt's house for the next three weeks. The bullet had just missed his heart, apparently because it had glanced off of one of the broken ribs he had. The gangsters that had tried to kill him had effectively saved his life by beating him before they shot him.

Irony hurt...

It was another week before he was up and moving around like normal; well, almost normal. His chest still hurt every now and then. Every time he would take a deep breath a stabbing reminder of the bullet that had almost taken his life would flare up. It would be a long healing process, and his therapy would be filled with blood.

When Jack was OK to leave the house, he made his way back to his. School was no longer even the remotest thought in his mind; his life had now taken a different direction.

He walked into his house and made his way to his room. He had had weeks to think about this.

He opened his closet and pulled a black long sleeve t-shirt and his black leather jacket from inside and laid it on the bed. Then he walked back and reached down, pulling his black Doc Martin's out and setting them next to his jacket. He turned and made his way to the hall closet and slowly opened the door. He reached inside, and pulled out the black carbide machete his father had bought for him in his last birthday, and the black, faceless mask his dad had worn the last Halloween to scare kids when he opened the door to give out candy.

He brought the rest of his new outfit into his room and set it on the bed, where he stared at it for quite some time, and then glanced at the Punisher poster on the wall, and steeled himself for what he was about to do.

He slowly undressed, and then reached into his dresser, pulling out a pair of black Dickies pants and slipped them on. He then methodically donned the rest of his outfit, and made his way to the living room where he set the mask and his machete next to the front door, and went outside to the garage. He opened the door and stepped in. There was a ten-gallon gas can his father kept for the generator they used when camping. He picked it up and made his way to the gas station on the corner and filled it. Then he walked back to his house.

You do not own this city.

He set the can down and made his way to the couch, where he sat for the next nine hours, waiting, planning.

When it was three o'clock in the morning he

stood and made his way to the front door. He set the gas can on the porch, strapped the machete to his back and slipped the mask in his back pocket.

Jack turned to stare into his house once more, and whispered, "I love you dad," then slowly closed the door and locked it.

He turned and grabbed the gas can, silently making his way down the street in the direction of the house occupied by the main group of gangsters that ran Coronado Street.

When he was a half a block away he stopped. He stared at the house a short distance away and took a deep breath, pulling the mask from his back pocket, and slipped it over his head. Then he bent down and picked up the can and made his way to the house.

As he approached it was quiet. At this time of the night everyone was asleep.

He made his way through the yard, and removed the cap from the can, and walked the perimeter of the house, dousing the base and sides with the petrol.

When he finished his circle he walked up the front stairs and grabbed the doorknob. He paused and turned it slowly. It opened.

Good.

He slowly entered the house, and scanned the living room. He saw two people sleeping on the couch; a guy and a girl, and the gangster that had shot him passed out in a recliner with an almost emptied forty hanging limply in his grasp. CSL was tagged in large letters across the wall behind the recliner. Coronado Street Locos.

You're about to see what loco truly is, Jack silently thought to himself, his eyes pulling to a squint behind his mask.

He turned and made his way into the kitchen where he quietly splashed the flammable liquid across the walls. He used a cup to make sure it was spread thoroughly, and then walked back to the living room.

He crept silently behind the couch, and circled the room, leaving a liquid trail behind him, and then made his way to the stairs leading up to the second floor.

He walked up the stairs, dousing the carpet that covered them as he did, ensuring nobody would be using them to exit from above, and then set the can on its side at the top, its remaining contents spreading outwards in a pool around it.

He walked back down the stairs, and made his way in front of the one who had said that he had shot his father, and then pulled his machete from his back, and kicked his feet off the ottoman.

"What the fuck?" the gangster said as his eyes came to focus on the faceless visage cloaked in black standing in front of him.

"You killed my dad," Jack said, raising the machete into the air, and bringing it down in a fast arc, the blade burying deep into the side of the man's skull with a wet thud.

There was a scream from behind him as the girl that had been sleeping on the couch woke up to find a figure in black looming over the still twitching corpse of her friend, his blood spritzing out in a crimson, pulsed arc.

Jack turned slowly, yanking the blade out of the bald man's skull, a stream of burgundy liquid shooting across the wall behind the man as he did, blood splattering across the graffiti in a fitting display of what was about to come.

She continued to scream as the man beside her shot up, his eyes darting wildly back and forth before coming to rest on Jack. "What the—"

His sentence was cut mid-way through when he saw his friend lying lifeless on the recliner across from him, blood showered across the wall and puddling beneath the chair. He stood and rushed Jack, who side stepped quickly and brought the blade hard across his back. The girl had run up the stairs, screaming to the others.

The gangster Jack had just butterflied fell hard against his friend corpse and hit the floor, writhing in pain from the inch deep gash running from his right shoulder to his left hip.

Jack stepped towards him slowly and lifted the blade up. He recognized him as the one that had hit him first in the alley. "Looks like you're the one that won't be calling the cops now, *puto*," he said, placing the blade against his neck and pushing forward.

The man twitched, his arms and feet flailing as the room filled with the sound of gargled gasps.

Jack twisted the blade slightly, and then yanked it back, spraying his legs with the warm life that filled the gangster.

As he turned to make his way to the stairs, one of the gangsters from above reached the bottom and pointed his pistol at him.

Jack dove backwards behind the couch as five shots rang out, reverberating through the living room, and filling his ears with a slight ring.

He lay there for a moment before another two shots rang out, and then a smile crept on his face beneath the mask.

He reached into his pocket and pulled out a lighter. He rolled it in his hands for a second, the smile growing larger before flicking it to life, and touching the small dancing flame to the glistening wet spot on the carpet in front of him. It instantly ignited, sending a blue and white snake slithering towards the center of the room. A moment later the house was filled with a roaring light, and Jack stood quickly, rushing towards the man that was overcome with the fact that the world around him and just ignited into a raging inferno.

He yelled, and then swung hard, bringing the blade of the machete against the side of the man's neck. The arc was only slowed slightly by the man's spinal cord. Then his head fell to the carpet with a soft thump.

He looked up as the same feeling he had felt in the alley repeated itself four times in his chest.

He heard the pops, but by the time his brain connected the sound and the feeling, he realized his legs had given out from beneath him and he fell to a heap on the floor. He had been shot. He had been careless.

As he lay there feeling his shallow breath beginning to fade, he heard the screams of the men at the top of the stairs as the snake reached the overturned can, and a fireball blasted through the hallway above.

Darkness moved in around him, and as the sounds of screaming, and burning faded away, he realized that he still had a smile on his face.

* * *

The yellow plastic tape fluttered softly in the wind; the words, *police line do not cross* flitting back and forth on the breeze. Behind the citrine ribbon, the burned husk of a two-story building loomed blackened and menacing. The acrid smell of smoke was gone, and all that remained of the raging inferno from a week prior was a black and grey frame with a collapsed roof.

Inside what had been the living room, there was nothing but ash and exposed pipes. The carpet had been reduced to charred floorboards, and there were white markers where the coroner had assumed the bodies had lain; arson they had assumed, no investigation due to the address, and the people that had inhabited it. Twelve in all.

At the foot of the stairs there was a small pile of ash, and the top of it was stirring, as if a soft breeze blew across it.

Out of the pile a single red ember rose lazily into the air; it was followed moments later by another. One after another, the flitting embers rose upwards towards the sky, and soon the pile appeared to be shifting form, like a carbonized log shifting from the heat in a campfire, crumbling in reverse.

As the cinders made their way towards what used to be the ceiling, the pile of ash began to take form; like the preserved remains from Pompeii, the form of a person curled up took shape.

The embers became light sparks, small tufts of

smoke making their way upwards, in a delicate dance with the floating sparks, and then a face formed, and the eyes shot open; Jack's eyes.

Also by **Donald Morrison**

Rabid Lands

The Journal

Ouroboros

Grey Zone

Dawn of the Magi

Revelations

The Last 21

The Isle of Children

ENTITY

Deadslayers